LITTLE TALES OF FAMILY AND WAR

1990-1999

MARTHA KING

Spuyten Duyvil
New York City

ISBN 1-881471-47-0
       1-881471-48-9 (hdc.)

Cover, frontispiece and ornaments © 2000 Basil King.
Cover Painting: *Aggie & Bill*, oil on canvas, 9' X 7', 1971-2.

Grateful acknowledgement to the editors who previously published the following: *First Intensity*: "The Mad Shitter's Daughter", "Babs", "Craft"; *Bomb*: "The Life of a Liar", "Family Plots"; *Anatomy RAW*: "Recognition"; *Zealot Press*: "Subway", "Porn Theater" (both in *Monday Through Friday*); *New Rivers Press*: "Little Photograph" (in *The Taking of Hands*).

Spuyten Duyvil
P.O. Box 1852
Cathedral Station
NYC 10025
http://spuytenduyvil.net

Library of Congress Cataloging-in-Publication Data

King, Martha, 1937-
       Little tales of family and war, 1990-1999 / Martha King.
       p.cm.
       ISBN 1-881471-48-9 (hdc.) -- ISBN 1-881471-47-0 (paper)
       1. United States--Social life and customs--20th century--
Fiction.   2. Domestic fiction, American. I. Title.

       PS3561.I4817 L58 2000
       813'.54--dc21
                                                              00-025118

To my dear and my dears, again.

CONTENTS

CASTE

Matthew left town every fall for an eastern prep school. He came home for vacations with great jokes, stories about Boston or New York, and new tunes on his classical guitar. Matthew knew the difference between a fugue state and a fugue in Bach; he spent a summer at a Quaker work camp in Indonesia; he read poetry. He had long legs and grey eyes. He was perfect. He had a girlfriend named Katherine who went to prep school too and was as perfect as he.

Matthew grew up to be a hematologist and married her. Last year he took a morphine overdose two weeks after learning he had cancer. He and Katherine hadn't been able to have children, which they adjusted for as civilized people should. But their adopted son gave up struggling to pass high school and married at seventeen. He was working as a motorcycle mechanic.

"A good man," Matthew said, with helpless distance. "I respect him very much."

Every summer vacation, Matthew used to show me a short story. He'd have used another fictional technique but the plot never changed: a white teenager paints yellow deck chairs brown. The retarded son of a black handyman plays nearby. When the job is done, the white youth removes brown paint stains from his hands with benzene, goes into the house a minute, and returns to find the little boy rubbing at his brown hands with the benzene rag.

Nothing Matthew did with this story satisfied him.

"What did you hope would happen?" I asked the last time he ever showed it to me.

UNFINISHED PLOTS, AGAIN

"...since the events in a script are expected, they are themselves uninteresting. That is to say, it is the unexpected obstacle or distraction that merits description and interests a reader. When people read stories that are constructed to contain equal numbers of routine (script-based) actions, interruptions, and irrelevant actions, the interruptions are recalled best of all. Readers regard the interruption of a script as the whole point of the story."

—Authors' names misplaced

Clipped from an article in *Science* describing a study of memory and cognition.

For example:

A TOBACCO FARMER IS BITTEN BY A STRANGE WORM....

A middle-aged homosexual adopts the nephew of one of his lovers. An informal adoption. The boy is about fifteen. He's a street kid, out of the Bronx slums. He showed up one evening at his uncle's house, running away from a family broken by drinking, drugs, and mental weaknesses. His uncle is living on a farm owned by two actresses, one of whom is making a great deal of money in made-for-TV movies. His lover, the man in our story—let's call him Roger—lives in a small town nearby, where he runs a mail-order book-search service. Roger wins the boy with promises that he will never desert him, as the uncle surely will, and soon. After all, the uncle is involved in getting his living by being useful to these two actresses, and generally to people with money and unorthodox needs. However, the clash over the boy ends the uncle's friendship with Roger.

Roger tells his friends this opportunity for fatherhood fills an aching gap in his life. The arrangement is absolutely not about sex he asserts. But it is. He entertains his friends with breathless reports about the boy's predatory behavior with the local girls. Everything is important: the speeding tickets, telephone messages, bouts with crabs, the strategies he uses on the girls, the fights he has with their parents, uncles, and older brothers.

Some of Roger's friends are tolerant, others bored, and one or two denounce Roger as irresponsible. He's unperturbed. He carefully does nothing to spark the boy's interest in a wider world, to help him find something to do or be as he grows up.

As time passes, the boy comes to realize the power of his situation. He doesn't have to work, go to school, do household chores. In fact, Roger enjoys bragging about his irresponsibility.

"He's not housebroken," Evelyn complained in her whiskey baritone. The boy interrupts conversations, holds his fork in a fist, shoves his plate away and leaves the table as soon as he's full.

By the time the boy is a young man who vacillates between puppy-dog cheerfulness and menacing sullenness, friends have begun avoiding Roger. "He's just a kid," Roger brags. When he's barraged with demands for money, Roger still says, "For god's sake, he's just a kid!" Roger manages to cast himself as infatuated, obsessed; he presents himself, subtly, as a victim. Some of his friends believe it and discuss Roger's victimization behind his back.

"If you love him, you have to take him as he is," Roger says. He's sure that no one knows he has no feelings for his ward at all.

If it were up to me, I'd make this outcome riven with lightning bolts, random, heavenly disaster, which shows you how vengeful and vindictive I can be. One might suspect I'd been a neglected child myself.

TWO JAPANESE BROTHERS GROW UP IN ALBANY....

A woman who works in a jewelry store sells a customer her own wedding ring.... She is Heather's mother. Heather said the marriage between her mother and father is fine. She said it was a fairly good quality diamond. She said the customer possibly thought the ring was being modeled. Heather said, "She was offered a really good price."

Heather, who works in my office, gave me a quizzical look as I swallowed hard. She told the story while several of us stood around the coffee machine.

Were we talking about robberies, weddings, or stock market prices? I can't remember. The story seemed to come out of the blue. But nothing does.

A WOMAN FORCES HER NEXT-DOOR NEIGHBORS
TO ADOPT HER DOG....

A restless young man has a summertime fling and learns later about the life of his son.... The fling is in Provincetown in July and most of August. Our young man is nineteen, contrary and rebellious. He would like to be serious, and eventually he will become so, but at this time, he's simply uncomfortable. He is also anxious, wild, and smitten with words. She's the daughter of a hugely wealthy family whose firm manufactures one of the world-recognized symbols of

American life. Blue jeans. Jello. Coca Cola. She's eighteen, tan, long-legged, adventurous, and smart. It's Romance.

They part as summer ends—which they had both expected to do. But early in October she writes to say she is pregnant. The letter is straightforward: she needs nothing but feels honor-bound to tell him that she has decided to continue the pregnancy and keep the child. It's an act out of the very confidence that had attracted him to her. He is ashamed and estranged, from himself and from her. He never answers the letter.

Within a few years he has married a woman who seems much more like himself—uncertain, angry, and wistfully ambitious for a life in art. Soon they have a baby, then another. Their marriage doesn't work well, but in time it does bring home to the man—as he approaches thirty—that the difference between himself and his wife is like the gap between himself and the art he would like to make. This acknowledgement spurs him to begin the hard labor of creating a new, more disciplined self.

In the midst of the ugly divorce that followed, he receives a letter from his now twelve-year-old son. "I would like to see you," the letter says. It is as straightforward as the letter his mother had written announcing her pregnancy. The man is in the process of leaving his wife and younger children and cannot answer this letter either, although he knows another chance is very unlikely.

He told me this long story with regret and acceptance and the ease born of practice because he's told this story to other people before me.

I was leafing through a news magazine the other day when I saw my old friend's strong cheekbones and characteristic eyes in a picture of a man who had just taken over a famous family corporation. He had his arm around his son, a boy of seven; a littler girl was sitting on his lap smiling and glowering at the same time. Her brows were knit together in a stubborn look that's been familiar to me for 30 years. I was surprised to be so shaken and so surprised, and I peered closer and closer at my friend's grandchildren—colored dots in a magazine.

This collection seems to need a final story, as if these interruptions can themselves be interrupted or explained. Scientists who need random numbers for certain experiments complain that nothing emerges from disorder without acquiring order on the way.

THE MAD SHITTER'S
DAUGHTER

When coffee was served her dad would start up. Stories doing all the work that stories do. Gather round me hearties, gather round, they begin. Oh, my best beloved. Hear and remember. A story I heard, a tale I invented, a history I say happened to me.

Outside New York City, supermarkets come in sizes that stun us Manhattanites. There are stores out there with aisles wider than Broadway, gargantuan rows devoted to cornflakes. We're like tourists from Iron Curtain Europe before the fall, or like Europeans facing Paul Bunyan. Not only the size of the stores, but the size of the containers in which food is sold! Do they eat all this?

My boss who runs conferences popped into one of these markets somewhere in Cleveland; it was raining and the local organizers had miscalculated on food for the coffee breaks. She grabbed two gallons of milk and a tin of Oreos.

It was, she said, about the size of a laundry basket. A man behind her in the express line seemed to be staring out at the rain lashing the plate glass while her purchases slid toward the bagger.

"Hey," he said, "can I come home with you?"

My stories are often stolen—correction—appropriated. How could there be art without larceny? Or stories? Or language? In larceny, the entries are erased, the diary written after the fact, and all thievery left raw. Later, scholars may trip on discrepancies and torture themselves to reconcile the accounts. Without larceny, how would there be history?

The aircraft carrier had a huge phone system, her dad explained. So the phone would ring the captain while he was eating dinner.

"Captain, I'm going to shit on your bunk," the voice would say.

Crew dispatched at full speed.

Arrival in state room—too late!

The Mad Shitter had struck again. Turd on the pillow. (Had he squatted there to produce it or was it delivered?) This went on for months, and no culprit was found. Only shit. On the bedspread. On the shoe stand. In a dress hat. Only phone calls in a flat voice.

How was it done! Keys? Accomplices?

Her dad was in trouble for this, for that. He was always losing the little rank he acquired. The time was Cold War, and consumption was the major goal. Military budgets had to be justified, and long training cruises helped. Her dad was Cuban and suspected of communism. He was athe-ist and enjoyed the company of gay men. His head was shaved for something he did, and, "Oh!," he would tell his dinner guests, "if only I could have been the Mad Shitter's manager!"

How will the noose be tightened—what is funny squeezed out and what is terrible left to incubate? Will the phone ring? Will the daughter find out for sure?

"I'm sure he would tell me. He's old now and I'm grown. But he always says he doesn't know who it was. He says he never found out."

Is this my father? Am I his child? And did this story happen at all?

He has post office business several times a week as there are always letters and packages to France or Canada or Great Britain. No matter how hard we try to keep stocked with stamps, the packages have a way of hitting a sum we can't reach or divvy out. Then he will sigh and volunteer (again).

He hates to wait. I mean he truly hates to wait and seems to have no gift for that resigned alpha-wave state most people who wait can move into. But he's wonderful at patterns. He plans his post office visits like raids, timed for windows of opportunity, the lulls between traffic. Even so, yesterday when he found the lobby vacant, he was stunned. It was mid-morning just after a holiday, and he was braced for a jam of postal-starved neighbors.

A totally empty silent lobby. A luscious hot-sun blue-sky summer day outside. Every cage in the lobby was also empty.

"Is anyone home?" he called out.

"Oh hi," said the first clerk after a minute. "We wuz in back. It's been twenny-five minutes without a soul. We took a bet. First guy in here we'd ask to the beach."

"Ya ready?" asked clerk two.

They are all Puerto Rican housewives. Big women, with eye make-up.

"We split for tha watah, we pick up tha bee-ah?" said the third.

"Yes, maa-am!" he said, handing his packages onto the scale, as the lobby doors began swinging and people poured in. Six people. Nine people. The women's giggling shut down like a trunk lid.

"Shee-yut," muttered the one sticking stamp tapes onto his packages. Bam, bam, bam, she punctuated with her red first-class stamp. "Youda come, wouldn'tja? I wuz ready."

When he turned to leave there must have been twenty-two people in line, all fidgeting, daydreaming. And later that morning, the line snaked all the way back to the stamp machine, the one with the sticker that says "Save Time" and always blinks "Out of Order" in L.E.D. green.

If you are waiting for explicit messages, remember the rule: mocking the storyteller risks dissolution. The world is a story we agree on. The Mad Shitter smiles. He has bamboozled everyone.

COHERENCE IN DOCUMENTS

LETTER TO JIM HAINING, SALT LICK PRESS,
AUGUST 25, 1998

"The postcard you sent of the church in Green City, Missouri, is a treasure: stark American folk architecture at its finest. Did you notice that the legend, in ink on the actual photo from which this postcard was made, reads "Babtist Church"—exactly as pronounced?

"The old family photos all share the eerie resonance of that common urban sight: one empty shoe in the middle of the street. There are no names on them; nothing is written on the backs. Who are these people and how do we come to hold their likenesses?

"I inherited several boxes and albums of photos of this period from my Lynchburg, Virginia grandmother. She'd gotten them when someone died, but again no one had ever written on the backs except for one or two cryptic legends: 'Sarah,' or '1891'. No one in my living family has the slightest idea who these people are.

"The best item is a double portrait. An embossed leather-backed folder, which opens to show two portraits in oval frames. One is a young man with chin whiskers; the other the same man older, with a huge black beard. This note was folded up inside: 'Father taken in the 1850s. When he left for the Army in 1861 his beard was like this. He came home on leave a year afterwards and was full-bearded and moustache (sic). He never shaved after his return.'

"Like most Southern families we have had several devoted genealogists, so I know for sure that only three of my relatives were actually in the Civil War: my maternal great-grandfather Theodore Shuey, who fought on the Union side; my maternal great-great-grandfather William Mays, who didn't survive (it's unclear which side he fought for; some in the family say he didn't fight at all, but caught the pneumonia that killed him while hiding out in a swamp); and my paternal great-grandfather T.N. Thompson. T.N. was just one year in the Army of Virginia. He 'didn't care for it' and his mother got him a job with the railroad instead, is what the family always said.

"The man in the double frame isn't any of them. But he sure looks like a study in post-traumatic stress syndrome. Even hidden by the hat and huge beard, you can see his post-war eyes are mad.

"Thanks for sending the package. It reminded me that I've been stalling about working on a piece about family. Starting with my grandmother Agnes, Aggie, my mother's mother. She was an artist, quite good at watercolor landscapes. Aggie taught me to say 'suffragist,' never 'suffragette' but lost her own struggle to take her work or herself seriously. Still, she taught herself Dutch so she could translate a collection of letters from Raden Kartini (1879-1904), a Javanese feminist. The resulting book, *Letters of a Javanese Princess*, was published in England in 1921; it went back in print in the U.S. in the 1960s, with a preface by Eleanor Roosevelt, and might be around even now, as it sounds a lot of current themes.

"It's hot here too...makes me ramble...."

My mother, Isabella, left a paper accordion folder, labeled in pencil, "Letters, from studio desk, January 1936". Here's one, on the following letterhead:

Shuey & Company (Incorporated),
Analytical and Consulting Chemists,
115 East Bay Street,
Savannah, Georgia;
Official Chemists:
Florida Pebble Phosphate Export Association
Florida Hard Rock Phosphate Export Association

Pet is my grandmother Agnes; the writer is her brother, my great-uncle, Philip Shuey. They are the children of Theodore Frelinghuysen Shuey, of Churchville, Virginia, in what everyone calls the Valley of Virginia.

"March 30th, 1935.

"Dearest Pet: I have really no time to write now as I am in a hurry to get to Bluffton.... I am so sorry about the present crowd of tenants turning out badly too. I am sorry you have to go on a trip to get property straight and hope you can arrange to sell it. I have some nibbles on my property and am making a drive to sell it within a couple of months. It is hard though for me to do much on account of being busy....Unless one keeps on jacking up the agents, it is very hard to make them do anything.

"Can you make out all right with your finances, I mean with regard to your New York trip? I have an awful lot of expenses on me, but want to do what I can. Mama may be writing you about being hard up, but she is having more done for her than ever. She doesn't realize it because she gets money in installments so as to keep her from 'blowing it in' on all sorts of unnecessary things.

"I surely am sorry about the tooth. Unless an abscess has progressed too far it can be cured, and the tooth saved by what is known as 'ionizing', which is done by a weak electric current working on added iodine to the affected part. The iodine is ionized and this is a purification and sterilization process... my dentist told me that a great many people could have their teeth saved by this treatment.

"Don't pay any New York dentist any big fabulous price: $15 to $20 is plenty. I think it only cost me about $10.

"I have a friend in New York who is a biochemist and I am sure that she could be of help to you. Her name is Mrs. Pauline Van Alstyne. She is at the New Weston Hotel, 34 East 50th Street. She is very bright and clever and I know you would like to meet her anyway, aside from assistance she can render regarding doctors. Her husband died from an infection after they were married just a year. She is very well traveled.

"Am so sorry that one of the Wright boys died. He was buried today, was brother to the one in Billy's class, who himself is not well. He died from an infection. A sister (the only one) died from about the same thing about six years ago. His father was a friend of Jim's. [Jim is Agnes's husband, James Keith Symmers, my mother's father, the grandfather I never knew.] They had had law business together in New York and Mr. Anton Wright spoke so highly of Jim. He married a Miss Smythe from Charleston—cousin to my Prof. Smythe of V.P.I., and also cousin to Col. Johnson's widow (also a Smythe). Col. Johnson was from Cismont and was commandant of cadets at V.P.I. for a long time. He had a nervous breakdown and after the doctors told him he had to get away from his work a year (he was teaching math and other subjects at V.P.I.) he collapsed by shooting himself. This happened about a year and a half ago. Then soon after that his brother in Birmingham, who was my room-mate my postgraduate year, did the same thing....

Affectionately, Phil"

My father, Lambert, left a green metal file stuffed with manila file folders. In the one, which he labeled "John Thompson I" there are multiple copies of deeds recorded in Hanover and Louisa counties, Virginia, and at least twenty copies of letters from my great-grandfather, my grandfather, and my father all trying to trace the origin, birthplace, or identity of one John Thompson (John Thompson!) who bought (or rented? an annual "Fee Rent" of one shilling is mentioned on some of the photocopied papers) for 40 shillings, 400 acres of Hanover County, Virginia, in 1736. But other papers say it is uncertain what county the land was in as new counties were added to the state in the early 19th century and many boundary lines were redrawn.

The 40 shilling price seems definite even if it isn't clear if it was the purchase price or a kind of deposit/escrow. Various handwritten copies of the contract agree that at least three acres of every 50 had to be "cultivated and improved" within three years or "estate would cease" and the land would be given to someone else. That would be 24 acres total. Bringing 24 acres under cultivation in that amount of time with the technology of the period would have been quite a job if this land was virgin—forested and never farmed before. On the other hand, the land might well have been brutally lumbered, abandoned and weeded over. It had already been 110 years since Europeans first came to Piedmont Virginia.

It's clear my grandfather worked on the problem of identifying John Thompson from at least 1937 until senility took him in the late 1950s. Then my father took up the chore. "Out of a sense of filial piety," he writes in several of his letters. The documents relating to this search trace different states of craving for information. My great-grandfather and my grandfather's letters are mostly addressed to county courthouses. My father's go there too but also seek academic help from the Virginia State Library, the library at William and Mary College, and the Society of Genealogists in London. In the mid-1980s, as macular degeneration and mental decline "which was caused, we believe, by transient ischemic attacks or mini-strokes" combined to blunt his abilities, he abandoned the work. He died in 1993, at the age of 88.

Filial piety is not what I ever observed in him. When I was a child, I thought he seemed obligated. As an adult I detected a distinct hint of internalized coercion and I might use the word intimidated. For example, he had us three children baptized and somewhat regularly sent to Sunday school when we were small, despite Isabella's total lack of enthusiasm for anything related to church. He made her do it. So she got us there, dropped us off, and would be there to pick us up when we came out. Lambert rarely, if ever, went to church himself during that time, and he didn't say he believed. Instead he defended the whole business to her—in our hearing—as "a child's need for ritual."

SIX OTHER FOLDERS IN THE STEEL BOX

Some are filled with photocopies of Thompson family wills written in 19th century handwriting, with transcriptions in early 20th century handwriting, and still later typewritten versions, dated in the 1940s. Some are carefully attached to the copies of originals. Many other copies are scattered throughout the folders. There are copies and copies and copies of the same documents. There are also affidavits by local court clerks verifying the names of people mentioned in the documents or the names of those who signed as witnesses to the copying.

Many hold letters to and from members of the Eubank family. Again, the topic is genealogy. These people seem gripped by a sense that they are at risk of forgetting who they were or where they came from. But Baz and I have spent a few hours writing out our family trees, and it's fascinating how just two generations, with a remarriage or two, can result in a confoundedly complicated and uncertain picture.

There are lists of Eubank children in these folders. Some are on the backs of envelopes, some on lined yellow legal pads. Many letters have been annotated and copied. For other people and then never delivered?

A letter from my grandfather, H. Minor Thompson, to "Cousin Edward" (Major Edward N. Eubank of Newport News, Virginia), dated 1943, typed from his dictation by his secretary at the Lynchburg, Virginia, City Tax Department (per the conventional initials at the bottom), urged Cousin Edward to make a will:

"I am making no suggestions as to whom you should leave your property. I am only urging that you express your wishes in this respect in a will.... I am attaching herewith a list of your nearest kin insofar as they are known to me. I think this family tree is correct, but I may be in error and you are probably the only one who can detect these errors....

"In trying to locate your next of kin I have omitted entirely any effort to locate any of the Lathams or Cannons, but in the absence of a will it would be the duty of your executor to trace all of your collateral kin so that their interests could be protected."

I'm not sure if this Cousin Edward is same person who wrote to H. Minor in 1937, in soft and elegantly readable 19th century script:

"Dear Minor: ...I am sending an old tin-type of Cousin Jennie taken in the early 60s, and also one of your father taken just at the time of his marriage. Give this last to Elise (H. Minor's eldest sister) with my love and compliments.

"The Eubank Bible is very large and heavy but I will send it to you as my tenure is short and you are practically the head of the Thompson-Ellis-Eubank et al. family. If I can pay the expressage I will do so. Postage is prohibitive. But I am afraid I will have to unload on you. A bank failure left me with a heavy burden and my pension barely keeps me going while endeavoring to pay something every month on this bank debt.

"Do not misunderstand me as making an appeal directly or indirectly. I mean nothing of the sort, as I have learned long ago that the Philosopher's Stone is 'Pay as you go.' If you cannot pay, do not go. And that's that.

"As opportunity permits I go over my accumulated junk pile and destroy everything personal. Anything of interest from a family standpoint I will send to you for 'reasons previously assigned.' Give my love to the household, especially the women-folk. P.S. If you should see Mrs. John W. Childs (the dear friend of my youth, Miss Luey Brown) tell her I think of her frequently and always with kindness.
Sincerely and affectionately—E. N. Eubank"

Yesterday, I dug this carbon copy out of the box—a 1953 letter from my grandfather, H. Minor Thompson, to the British Embassy in Washington:

"Back in 1941 when England was threatened with an invasion by Hitler I had the pleasure of contributing a shotgun and ammunition to the defense of England, which is evidenced by the attached papers. In due time I received an acknowledgement directly from England but the censor deleted the name of the recipient. Later on in the war I wrote the British Embassy in Washington reciting the above facts and told them that I would like to correspond with the British officer if his name could be supplied and gave them satisfactory evidence as to my character, etc. Within a matter of days I received a letter from the British Embassy furnishing the information requested and I had a very pleasant correspondence with Colonel Wheatly."

The rest of this letter is missing.

I can't find papers acknowledging receipt of the shotgun, but I did find the reply to this letter from the British Embassy in Washington, also dated 1953:

"As our wartime files are now put away in the archives, I have not been able to ascertain how the name of the recipient of your shotgun was so promptly sent you. I am returning your copy of the Lieutenant Colonel's letter herewith." The writer, (Miss) L. Johnston, then suggests that he write to the Library of Congress and the Society of Genealogists in London for the history of John Thompson. She added:

"P.S. Dorset is in the South West of England, and I enclose a travel folder on that section which you may find of interest."

Had Colonel Wheatly's letters been sent from somewhere in Dorset?

Would I snoop around Dorset looking for the Lieutenant Colonel Wheatly who served in World War II? And if I found him what would I say? "Was it a good gun?" or "Are you related to John Thompson who lived in Virginia in 1736?"

John Thompson! Why not try Tom Smith?

"Get a life," is what Ginger said when I told her about the box, the letters, and all the genealogic frenzy. "Didn't they have something better to DO?" she shrieked. Get. A. Life.

PAMPHLETS AND A HOMEMADE BOOKLET

I should tell Ginger that the box contained two privately printed genealogy pamphlets by people not in my family, suggesting that genealogy was a popular occupation. There's clearly a competitive spirit involved. People exchanged letters challenging each other's accuracy and recounting their researches in detail. Like stamp collectors, these practitioners believed there was some larger value to their passionate work. I should tell Ginger this is the lost world of the amateur scientist, the amateur historian, the amateur inventor—all of whom might do respected, ultimately essential work as a hobby. The 19th century was full of them.

The two booklets are heavily annotated by my grandfather, known to us kids as Big Minor. So is his collection of Southern history books. Books and booklets are stuck full of corroborating or supplemental accounts, human interest feature stories mostly, clipped from 20th century newspapers. The clippings are now dark yellow to deep orange to almost mahogany because of the high acid content in the paper. They've left acid stains on many pages. The paper clips have rusted and are embedded like old nails in a tree trunk.

The homemade pamphlet is a folio of legal-size paper printed in purple mimeograph, fastened with a brad. It contains the postscript: "The foregoing statement was made by Mrs. W.H. Kinckle...grand-daughter of William Thompson...for her daughter Grace Kinckle Adams, who has permitted the above copy" (certified with a rubber stamp: SEP 25 1913). It opens with this story:

"In the long time ago—what year I know not—A boy & girl were left orphans in England—(London I think), an Uncle in Virginia, America, hearing by letter of their sad condition, wrote to a friend to send them over the broad Atlantic to him, they commenced their journey——the passage across must have been very rough, for quite a good deal of their belongings was lost, and the boy died during the passage over. She lived with her Uncle. (I do not remember that I ever heard which it was, a paternal or a maternal Uncle.) One day she was gathering corn for dinner, she felt something hard in her shoe—hurt her foot very much—on investigation it proved to be a gold coin stitched between the sole and lining of the shoe—in both shoes there were several coins of some denominations sewed in for 'hard times'——her relatives or friends in England must have been well-to-do persons, for the legend goes these were satin shoes and only worn when rough ground had to be gone over——the rest of the time—for a while 'till shoes were brought from England she had to go bare-footed. A great many of her working clothes were lost in the storm, and the rest which were saved had worn out—her name was Jennie Gissage."

The rest of the booklet is devoted to accounts of deaths, each of which took place over a number of days. Each person described met death with identical Christian resignation. The prayers, descriptions of physical symptoms, and spiritual advice to the survivors go on for pages in the conventional elevated style of the day. In addition, there is a collection of descriptions of houses where various members of the Thompson family lived, but the names of neither counties, towns, or street addresses are included.

Two business documents in a folder relate to human slaves: one is an agreement between Charles P. Lee and S. Watson with a third person, whose name is obscured (B.J.?), for "the hire of a negro girl Amanda for the year 1852—the girl to be humanely treated—clothen in the usual manner & returned at the end of the year with good blanket & shoes." This paper is marked vertically "Received payment in full."

The other document is a memo, marked "Duplicate - Valuation of Negroes belonging to S.H. Thompson's children." It seems to be part of a will or a settlement and explains how various assets were to be divvied up. For example: "Stephen, 18 years old, and Wallace, 17, together valued at $718.50. One quarter of which went to be divided between H. Thompson and Richard Jordan, one fifth of which went to Mrs. Thompson, and the balance ($57.50) to S.H. Thompson."

After all of this is worked out with respect to "Mary and her 2 children George and Thomas, Nathan, and James, who was sold in 1839 for $875," there is an agreement signed by three Thompsons and witnessed by two more Thompsons that we "agree to hold the slaves in severally and to pay and receive the sums producing equally"—whatever that means.

Was Amanda a wet nurse?

Were Stephen, Wallace, Mary, Nathan, James, and the two children, George and Thomas, sent away to be sold in order to divide their value among the three Thompsons signing? The date is 1842. Three signatures. Beside each one, the word "seal" is handwritten surrounded by curlicues—an ink seal, a virtual seal, the pen's gesture. No wax.

A final item of note is a loose stamped envelope, postmarked 1953, and addressed Mr. Minor Thompson, Lynchburg, Virginia. It arrived.

E-mail from H. B., 1999:

"Those old-time Southerners were a bunch, weren't they? I'm always, for some reason, surprised at their grasp of the English language (well-evidenced in your older quoted accounts), their grammatical precision, and all those fancy flourishes. No one talks like that anymore, and the kids don't have a clue, sad to say. While I enjoyed reading the letters and other items in your account, I have to wonder if, outside the context of a complete memoir, they could hold the attention of readers not connected to your own family. Know what I mean?"

TO FIX SOMETHING OLD

"Oh history, that little conjectural science, that great art..."

—Dr. Abraham Pais,
a twentieth-century theoretical physicist,
also a historian; that is to say, he writes biog-
raphy. His books conjure in language the
nexus from which ideas emerged. This
moves in time both forward and back.

To think about how language moves I'm wondering
how it dissolves. In a churchyard wall in Paul I saw,
according to the metal plaque, the grave of the last
person to speak Cornish. The tourist books point it out too,
and the local stores sell postcards showing the church wall.

This bothers me, because surely it's buncombe. The
countryside surrounding Paul is everywhere populated.
Countryside is always a place where everyone knows who's
who. Not a person this old woman could speak with? No
word of Cornish left? This phrase means something else,
points to another meaning. Cornish was over years before
the old lady in the wall was born. Something more useful

replaced it, something the old lady knew too. Useful, of course, is a tautology, defined by the perceiver of use.

A huge needle-thin ruin occupies a hilltop near Elaine's house in Kent. It's simply called the Monument. She says no one anywhere remembers what the structure was—whether fort, shrine, great house—only that it's very very old. What's left looks to be at least sixty feet tall and is the corner of something. The fallen parts must have been carried off, for a stoneless meadow runs right up to the base.

I would guess that bits of those stones lined wells, foundations, walls, and chimney pieces for several dozen miles around and that many of these structures are in turn gone now. The countryside around Elaine's is everywhere populated. Some of the farms being worked today may well have been old when the Romans invaded and built the road that still goes straight through Aldington. The Basket People made containers for grain around here. During the Le Tene period, people here made huge metal cauldrons for beer. It's been a good place for growing food ever since the climate settled.

Remembering what that great stone structure actually was even after it fell down should have been as basic as knowing where the river goes, should have been a knowledge passed on along with all the names for usual things. But it's forgotten. This mystery—that the names for things can stop—requires some reflection. Why would you stop calling a road or a river by its name?

There is a great debate about repressed memories in both legal and psychiatric circles. That a name will mutate over time as speech habits alter, that's expected. But why would you never tell your kids or your new friends that the name of the mansion at the edge of the neighborhood park is Litchfield House? Are memories repressed or do people simply refuse to discuss them. And which memories? The terrifyingly forbidden longing? The terrifyingly hideous reality?

What's in my mind this morning from the story that runs on and on in it, almost like memory, is a persistent green door at the top of the path through the garden; the paint on the door is persistent. It's sticky because, years ago, the handyman thinned the paint with linseed oil. If you touch that door your finger whorls are perfectly revealed, and you will print them in dark green on the next light-colored surface you touch.

At least for now, students of brain chemistry propose that memory is not stored but remade at the moment of use, resembling sound which exists only as it vibrates. Memory is not in the brain the way data are saved to a floppy disk or carved on a Mayan stele. Memory is not about retrieval, which changes the notion of "repression". There are neural pathways that acquire the habit of vibrating a certain way from many subtly similar stimulations over time. The phenomenon makes the much-used memories the brightest and easiest to reassemble. Source and destination exist only as they vibrate.

But we knew that!

By the art of the century now passing.

Turn left up the stairs, walk through the studio, turn right for the bathroom door. Yes, the door squeaks, as remembered. The tongue-in-groove wood walls are yellow-white or yellowed white, and there are the rust-stained toilet, the claw-foot tub, the slanty casement window with its twisted metal catch.

Clearer minds than mine understood immediately that this place was never what I have been in the habit of remembering, but rather this image is a new bead on the string, remade in the moment, always altered and altering, and already over when it first begins to change. The objects on which familiarity insists print on pale surfaces. These are our standards. Don't lean too hard.

On the other hand, on these fragile phenomena hang all. Here twine the spectres of freedom and love, race hate, sex rage, empathy, identity, despair. Old baggages persistent enough to run easily far into the new 21st century, leaving spoor in wells and chimneys. Always altered and altering. Outworn and damaging but refusing to be left behind.

THE LIFE OF A LIAR

This began when I wrote a story about a boy sitting in a tree, smoking a cigarette. The tree was a beech, near his home, with a beech's smooth bark and many convenient crotches. The cigarette was a Chesterfield, stolen from his grandmother's black pocketbook.

I started with the bark, the smooth air, the elegant dizzying sensations of familiar tree and unfamiliar smoke, the color of the smoke. I tried to enter his imagination as he made slow holes in green leaves with the red cigarette coal and savored an intense conviction that he was invisible. And I realized the story begins with a descent.

I thought of type on the page actually sloping downward, or a taped voice that sinks steadily toward each terminal period. But stories proceed as water-walkers across the shimmering appearance, pillowed by surface tension. The darker it becomes the more ready we all are for a story.

A SECTION IN WHICH A STORY IS TOLD

Tom was very proud of his mother. He showed me photographs of her and told me her story. She'd left home on her own when she was twenty—having somehow made a connection with Mexican filmmakers. A photograph showed a fair freckled Irish girl, holding down the crown of a dark straw hat in one hand.

Her Spanish must have been terrific, because soon she was working as a script girl for one of Mexico's top film directors. She returned to New Orleans pregnant. The father was the director, who was married; it was 1937.

She moved back in with her widowed mother, and as soon as her boy was used to the bottle, she left him in her mother's care and went out to work. She managed to find a job as a typist. Soon she taught herself shorthand and was promoted to secretary. Tom bragged about how quick she was at everything she did.

On a whim, she entered a speed-typing contest, sponsored by a large business machine company. She won. Within a year she was a national speed-typing champion, clocked at 132 words a minute on a 1939 office standard. I wouldn't have believed anyone could type that fast on one of those old iron manuals but Tom showed me an ancient newspaper clipping, and there she was again—the same sideways smile though somewhat plumper in the face, sitting at a boxy-looking typewriter, with a headline proclaiming her feat. That year she accepted an offer from the business machine company and began to perform at conventions and speak at sales meetings.

By 1941, when Tom was four, she moved out of her mother's house, but she left him behind. She was traveling three or four times a month, and a child should be raised by family, she told him, not by maids or nannies. Tom said he learned how to read the calendar waiting for his near-magical trips to her apartment. He hated his grandmother. And his mother did too. She hated her mother, and she gave her her child. A sense of the war between his mother and grandmother was the earliest given Tom accepted about the world. Their acrimony flowed back and forth over his head, as uncontrollable as a tide. He had to accept it as he had to accept the choice that left him stranded and unwanted, the choice that transformed him from a boy into a burden.

With his grandma, he was called Tommy O'Rourke. He was aware early on that something was wrong with this name. He was expected to pray before each meal, to cross himself at bedtime, and to be considered a troublesome nuisance whom God had given his grandmother the patience to bear and the kindness to tolerate. She did what was necessary for him as if he were a boarder or a household animal. But he was never good, she let him know. He stayed out of her sight as much as he could, in the alleys and streets around her skinny clapboard house.

With his mother, he was Tom Ruiz, and sometimes, teasingly, Tomas. She read stories to him, tickled him when she helped him dress. She took him to restaurants and movies where he was the only child present—a delicious sensation. He was almost a grown-up with her, even before he was old enough for school. Their favorite game was for her to tell him what life would be when he grew up; it was a movie, with himself as the hero.

She showed him the father's name on his birth certificate. She taught him words in Spanish. But this Spanish father never visited or sent him anything, although she insisted firmly *Papi* knew all about him through photographs and letters. As if a wall watched him, he told me. "I always felt—I knew—there was another way to know everything that happens, a way most other people don't see. I learned a lot from that feeling," he said.

But that was later. When he was six and seven, he tried not to think about it.

The summer he was thirteen, his mother told him *Papi* had sent for him, and he was to go to Mexico.

I imagine his mother being very matter-of-fact. I imagine that she has been expecting this, planning for it, for a very long time. Tom, on the other hand, feels as light-headed as if he'd been struck. When he answers her questions he hears the words echoing inside his head before they exit.

His mother is now an executive, a vice president of sales. She's put on a great deal of weight and acquired the manner of a distinguished and unusual woman. She still travels a great deal. This invitation, his mother informs him, might change their plan to end Tom's life with his grandmother by sending him to "a good boarding school" when he finishes eighth grade.

"Your father is used to having people recognize him and give him his way. Remember that. The house is very big. It's a mansion, really. Don't gawk. It's your own father's house. Treat the servants politely, but don't be friendly. You will be given presents. Accept them with thanks, but no matter how expensive they are, don't be over-impressed. Be dignified. Be firm. Be pleasant. You may be introduced to important people—film stars and politicians. You won't know them, because they're all different in Mexico, but be respectful. Just as if you met Rita Hayworth or President Eisenhower. Keep in mind you are there to give your father a chance to know you. He has no other sons. The other children are all daughters."

She is matter-of-fact, but she doesn't quell her undertone of triumph, of vindication. She doesn't say your life will not be the same after this visit but she buys him new underwear, an expensive leather suitcase, a navy-blue linen jacket, tennis shorts, a grown-up's wallet, and he watches his old life sliding away.

This is Mexico City. A screaming babble at the airport. A chauffeur retrieves him from the customs line and propels him into a waiting limousine. Inside sits a thick-set stranger with dark skin and startling blue eyes. A gravelly voice. Very hard hands.

Tom's mouth is dry. He had imagined being greeted with a handshake quickly turning into a hug. Instead they sit side by side in leather cushions, in a dark wood-lined compartment, turning awkwardly to look at each other.

Your age? You do well in school? What is your best subject?

Thirteen. I don't know. Recess, maybe. Ha ha ha.

Recess? A set-back? I don't understand.

This is the first of Tom's language difficulties. He tries to explain and words rush out of his mouth like sand from a dump truck. Be dignified. Be pleasant. Be firm.

The limousine hisses through brilliantly lit streets and then along quieter darker roads, up and down hills. It is night. Tom's effort to speak is interrupted by an incoming call on the car's two-way radio, an exotic instrument, into which his father (his father!) shouts in Spanish.

Then they are "home." Behind a high tile-topped wall. On a driveway past great thickets of exotic leaves and lawns, a cluster of tennis courts under black-green sailcloth, the glint of a blue swimming pool illuminated in the dark. It is cold when they climb out of the car. Tom had imagined a place hotter than New Orleans—but there is chill rattling wind. He has gooseflesh inside his light linen jacket.

This is Elise (your father's wife), very elegantly and artfully blonde. Your sisters: three grown women, three, they tell him, of the five. Their names are given him in a tumbling rush. They bear him away. They talk. They hug him, pet his clothing, examine his hair, laugh, hug him again. An occasional English phrase surfaces like a bubble on the flood of Spanish. He is offered food, while they crowd about watching him, and he burns his lips on hot cocoa, and his ears burn, and he cannot hear very well, perhaps because of the plane flight, and yawns reflexively. He is taken away to bed by chattering maids, "propelled" is more accurate. Propelled away from Ruiz, away from the light and noise, to a high-ceilinged bedroom two flights above the main floor.

After that first evening, the family is never again all in the same room at the same time. Ruiz has just begun a new film, Elise explains. Sometimes Tom sees him hurrying in, met by Elise and servants, ushered into a room that is immediately closed on the flurry of his commands. He leaves for the studio when the sky is barely cold blue. The wheels of his heavy car crunch the gravel far below Tom's room. Lights shine glassily and are then extinguished, and the spaces melt back into the gray balances of silence.

Now, Tom is to know that he is extra, foreign, and unequivocally unwanted. In Ruiz's presence Elise is charming, even mildly flirtatious. In his absence, neither she nor any other member of the household speaks to Tom in English. He spends the daytime wandering about the property. The household goes on around him as if he were a rock in a river. Occasionally he encounters one of his half-sisters, who giggles or passes him without acknowledgement. He quickly comes to dread mealtime. The servants stare at him. His questions are answered in Spanish, and all conversation passes over him. More acutely he dreads night when his body betrays him and he dreams about girls whose bathing suits melt from their breasts, movie stars who call for his help, the creamy buttocks and bellies of his half-sisters. The maids who clean his room snigger as they strip the bed and scold him in rapid Spanish.

They talk about him all the time. He thinks. He's sure. Each passing maid scurries in her haste to be the first to tell where he is this time. He locks himself into his bathroom and masturbates, hoping desperately to use it up before he sleeps, but night comes, and he dreams his cock is as big as a telephone pole, that everyone sees it and laughs as he tries to keep his hands away—and he wakes up in a frenzy, having come on the sheets again. There is laughing outside his bedroom door. Is someone watching him while he sleeps? In the mornings he is exhausted. His bed stinks like seaweed.

Late one evening he runs downstairs and barges through the door of his father's study. "Please let me come with you tomorrow. I'll stand wherever you say. I won't move. Just let me come with you."

Tom had been braced for an angry rebuff but Ruiz appears touched—pleased by the boy's passion. He's sorry, he says, that his new film has taken so much from him, so many problems. He touches Tom's hair. He can come along in just a few days. Soon. A promise. I'll have time for you.

Does Ruiz tell his wife about this plan, about his concern for the boy?

That morning before light, a naked woman slides into Tom's bed and wakes him by taking his cock in her mouth. She hisses endearments at him, holding his face. Her tongue is a rose-red lizard. Her breasts balloon above him. His complicity is total.

"You go home now," Elise says. "This morning. Before I tell your father what you do."

And his initiation is complete.

A SECTION IN WHICH I APPEAR

Tom had many stories. Each was backed up by a photograph or a newspaper clipping, some document as fragmentary as a piece of the true cross. Was Ruiz real? Was he really Tom's father? I'm not sure why I think he stole this romantic history, for solace or for entertainment, but I did and do. On the other hand, I knew he was some kind of orphan, some kind of invention.

It was hot in New Orleans that summer. Home air-conditioners haven't been invented; movie theaters are "air cooled." So are barber shops and pool halls and the bus station downtown. Was he thirteen the summer he learned to con for cigarettes and Coca Cola, and to play pool, and to pick his pool partners, and take their money? I know him well enough to know that only the prospect of a sure thing thrilled him. He loved pool because he knew just what he was doing, clear as a ball sighted down a cue. He hated any gambling that involved uncertainty.

He told me he had learned early how to slip both his mother and grandmother by making each think he was staying with the other. They were so angry with each other they rarely spoke. He told me some of the ways he got money on the street, too—sexual favors for example, and I believed these stories. But he didn't tell me if he and his mother ever spoke about what happened in Mexico, or if he lied to her about it. As for the "good boarding school"—it ceased to figure.

Still I wonder why he really did those favors. What did he think about or look for in the bars and waiting rooms where he soon began to live. There are some things one never tells to be believed when one lives the life of a liar. Tom called it "in the life" and it was in the life that he was able to go on. In most of his stories, he did it very well. He was all golden hair, rough trade aura, pulp romance adventure. As keen as any sports hero about the pain he could give and the pain he could endure. I believed most of this. In fact I learned quite a bit about the allure of male homosexuality—the combativeness, the thrills, the risk-taking—even the romanticized self-pity, though Tom wouldn't have liked me thinking that.

Unexpectedly, in one of his stories he was ill and hungry and scared. He was picked up by an old queen who took him home, fed him, nursed him through pneumonia, and then taught him muscle building.

"Homely old fag, but one hell of a coach," Tom said.

Old teacher, lost boy—it could have been a love story. But Tom seemed to believe the contempt he had for his rescuer was a required part of the relationship. Maybe it was. Tom enjoyed his contempt, his knowledge of the old man's need and paralyzed will. In those days, nothing seemed more pathetic than an aging homosexual, except, perhaps, an aging film actress.

There's another photograph accompanying this section: Tom, deeply tanned and hugely muscled, on the beach at Lake Ponchartrain, pulling the silky material of his trunks taut across his crotch with his forefinger and smiling down at the camera. And another newspaper clipping: "Junior Mister New Orleans Named"—with an account of a body-building contest. He was not quite sixteen. He was living in the French Quarter at the time, he said, in rooms that were, in terms of actual distance, quite near his mother's apartment.

She hired a private detective to find him.

He was confronted in a coffee house, eating a brioche.

"Complacency!" he laughed. "I never figured on her seeing all that Junior Mr. New Orleans stuff."

She marched him home. That was Tom's story: that he traded body building for gymnastics, finished high school requirements with a tutor, and won admission to this Southern university, famous for its liberal traditions, because of his athletic prowess. By the time I knew him he was twenty, and already a graduate student.

The athletic part was quite true: his specialty on the university gymnastics team was the horse. I used to go to the meets and he was wonderful to see—his biceps bulging and his powerful legs scissoring rhythmically first by his left ear, then by his right. His academic subject was French. I never heard him speak a word of Spanish. He was very proud of his Parisian pronunciation, and he liked to read the

French symbolist poets out loud to me, savoring the syllables.

"My advisor thinks I'm a genius because I know he's gay," Tom told me. His graduate thesis was an original translation of "Bateau Ivre", along with an essay about Rimbaud and the demimonde. "Piece of cake," said Tom, laughing at how hard other students had to labor for their degrees.

He often asked me to promise that I wouldn't tell anyone the things he told me, not even his friends. The oldest con in the world, he'd have pointed out. Our special secret. I can tell only you. Did he want me to break my word? I never did.

It was 1953.

My liberal college-professor father said "fairy", "pansy", or "fruit". In high school it was "queer" or "homo", and the thing was to lick your little finger and smooth your eyebrow with it. Literary college students avoided the slang and said "homosexual", carefully and a bit uncomfortably, unless they were speaking of homosexual women. Then the young men cheerfully said "lezzies" or "dykes", or with hostility, "bull-daggers" or "butches". Only Tom used the word "gay". He explained it to me as meaning rule-breaker, wayward in the sense of merrily deviant—an attitude that was, he pointed out, unheard of here among hayseeds and liberal suburbanites alike.

IN THE LIFE WHERE I WAS ABLE TO GO ON

That summer I lost my virginity to Tom and did line drawings to illustrate his Rimbaud manuscript. My models were Cocteau and Modigliani. Later, Tom had my drawings bound into the copy for the university library. They might be there still.

Who was this I in the Southern university town famous for its liberalism that I should have sought out such a young man and taken to the sensibility he shared with me?

This began when I wrote a story about a girl sitting in a tree, smoking a cigarette. The tree was a beech, near her home, with a beech's smooth bark and many convenient crotches. The cigarette was a Camel, stolen from her father's cache of cartons.

I started with the bark, the smooth air, the elegant dizzying sensations of familiar tree and unfamiliar smoke, the color of the smoke, and the girl's intense sensation of invisibility. She made slow holes in green leaves with the red cigarette coal. I thought of type that slopes down, or a taped voice that sinks steadily toward the terminal period. But stories are pillowed by surface tension and dart forward like pond-striders across the shimmering appearance.

Appearance is everything, my parents said. Where my mother was timid and fearful, she could appear dominant and confident. Where my father was jealous and resentful, he could appear thoughtful and even-handed. And when the outside world did not look the way they expected it to, they calmly refused to admit it.

I met Tom because my older sister was the student editor-in-chief of the university's literary magazine. Tom was poetry editor. I was seventeen, still in high school. I used to hang out in the Review office after school. My sister let me rummage through the pile of unsolicited manuscripts and read the truly awful stuff out loud for the entertainment of the staff. Then I paper-clipped them with rejection slips and tucked the pages back into their return envelopes. When the pile grew really large, spilling into the narrow floor space between the editors' desks, and the staff were frantic with proofing and trying to meet deadlines, I was recruited to make rejection decisions on my own.

Tom was not my sister's choice for poetry editor. The magazine was really run by a board of professor-advisors who doled out staff appointments to their favorite students. Thus the atmosphere in the Review office was frequently rank with competition and back-biting that reflected university department politics and sometimes the more personal ambitions and values of the students. My sister openly disliked Tom and was extremely annoyed at my interest in him. "He's a con man," she pronounced, accurately enough. I saw that she disliked him because she feared him. He radiated an interest in sex that was totally opposed to her ideal—that "that sort of thing" could and should be neatly sequestered in a designated corner of one's private life.

Tom took me into the town's underground.

The underground was a movable feast, a party somewhere different every weekend, a zone where genders blended, where divisions by academic discipline lost their importance, where correct public behavior was suspended. Everyone in the underground used code names, often feminized alliteratives of their real ones. The codes were for fun. The truth was everyone knew each other. But they frequently teased each other about "recking" or being "recked", which meant the use or threat to use an in-name in public.

Recking was meant to embarrass, but not expose. If it edged into threatening exposure the matter was very grave. Exposure could mean loss of career and livelihood for the mature; for students, expulsion; for everyone, an indelible social stigma. Exposure could even mean loss of liberty. Sodomy was a jailable offense in that state at that time, and the university was under chronic suspicion as a haven for homos and commies by conservative state legislators. There had been occasions when State Bureau of Investigation undercover agents had been deployed to get evidence on suspects who were university (and thus state) employees.

Not a single bar or restaurant in the town had a gay atmosphere or clientele. That was only possible at these parties, and attending them carried a risk. Nevertheless, there were many parties, and they were wild affairs; sometimes ebullient, sometimes hysterical, sometimes sad, occasionally dead serious or embittered, following changes in the underground's collective emotional climate. Ah, but the group! Business majors, star football players, old gentlemen from administration—all sorts of people I had identified as irredeemably square—would show up along with the actors and poets and graduate student aesthetes. The underground turned the world upside down for me, and I had yet another way to see that I was systematically lied to by my parents.

ANOTHER PERIOD PIECE AND ANOTHER SEDUCTION

There was a tree outside the window of the classroom that she took solace from. She looked at it so often and so long, she had a catalog of images: how the shine of bark changed from 2:15 to 2:50; the exact alterations in color if the rain were a mist-drizzle or a steady sluicing cold fall. Class time was memorable only as bark-time until the new French teacher arrived, the substitute mid-semester replacement for Mrs. Marchant, who had to leave when her husband had a stroke.

The new teacher was a stocky fireplug of a young man, his face scarred by acne, his eyes watchful and quick. This was his first teaching post, his first chance to work with kids without the intrusion of mentors and observers. Mr. Dixon broke decorum on his very first day; he took the opportunity to tell the class about himself. He was a Korean War vet. His war wound and his vet benefits had given him something he had never imagined earlier in his life—time to read, occasion to reflect, funds to go to college. It meant he could leave the back-labor ethos of his beleaguered ne'er-do-well family. He was not Southern. He was Boston Irish, slum born and bred for three hard generations since the 1848 potato famine. He knew quite a lot about the potato famine. He was short and harsh and unbelievably eager for his high-school students to like him. They didn't.

The bigger, poorer, more "male," students defected first. "Why's he always whining?" Don asked in the hallway, kicking his dark green metal locker door shut. "Shee-uuh! Him'n his damn poday-tahs."

"Go ahead, don't be scared," Mr. Dixon said the next day, demonstrating the French "u" by pursing his meaty lips. "U, U, U! Think of *puke,*" he grinned wickedly. "You wouldn't say *pook* would you?" Big Tee was sullen and embarrassed. No power on earth could make him make such a suggestible spectacle of himself as to purse his lips and say that fruity French "u" and everyone in class was on his side. He and Don exchanged conspiratorial looks. She began to watch Mr. Dixon, the turn of his hips, the thick black hair on his hands.

She knew she was cooked the day he told the class about his marriage. On his wedding night, he said, he told his wife "Je t'adore," and she answered, "Shut it yourself. What do you think I am?" He didn't seem to have the slight-est idea what he was saying—that that was probably the truth about what was going on between them.

The guy had gone and married a girl from the very neighborhood he said he wanted to leave, she reflected. It was as if the new self he invented in the veteran's hospital was so clear and inevitable to himself, it never occurred to him that anyone who knew him wouldn't see and believe it as well.

It was exactly the same in school. Racine. Moliere. He acted as if no one had ever encountered them before him—and that every high school kid who took a moment to listen would now become as excited as he was.

"Listen, class, listen!" he croaked, and he would walk as he read out loud, with a deliberate exaggerated foreign pronunciation. "What do you think, guys? I know you don't know this vocabulary yet, but listen to the rhythms."

She locked eyes with him, felt heat rise, and quickly shifted to the books on her lap. She was surprised how much his thick body and his stupidity excited her. He wanted her to stay after class; he wanted to know what those books were, those non-school books she snuck onto her lap. Black nihilistic energy snaked out of these books to comfort her: Camus, Jacques Prevert, plays by Bertholt Brecht. She had just started reading *Portrait of the Artist*. Books clutched to her chest, she asked why he wanted to know. She was not going to offer him anything!

His flirtation was as blunt as he was; there was no teasing play-pretend like Mr. Ender's banter when the girls in science lab balked at cutting their frogs. There was no dramatic exaggeration, the way Mrs. McAllister leered at the boys in her social studies class. Mr. Dixon didn't say a word but his aura was unmistakable: he wanted to fuck her right now, right here!—how about under the desk?—and he would have latched the door of the classroom on the smallest signal from her. Would he? Did he really know what he was doing? She was pudding; she was custard; she was tingling so violently she could barely walk away; she almost groaned out loud. It had not been like this with Tom.

She decided. She cut French the next day, but on Thursday she went, demure as a Dresden shepherdess throughout the period. If he also avoided eye contact with her, she had no way to tell for she never looked up. She knew it didn't matter. She waited for him in the dusk by the gate to the faculty parking lot. She had to tell him where to drive.

He was wild, desperate, and far too fast. He had not slept with his wife in six months, he said. Had she read *The Stranger*? Why was she interested in Jacques Prevert? In less than twenty minutes he was rooting for her again, pinching her nipples, shaking the little Chevrolet, and making her squeal with excitement.

Then he wept. He mopped his eyes on his necktie. He promised to make it up to her. Was she all right? What had he done?

"Can you do it again?" she asked. "I'm supposed to be home for dinner at 7:30 but I don't want to stop yet."

"Jaysus," Mr. Dixon said. "Jaysus. What are you, seventeen?"

"Eighteen," she said.

"How many guys you been with?" he asked in a garbled tone. And then, gaining some composure: "Jaysus. At least I didn't take your cherry."

"You'd hardly have known if you did," she said.

"I better drive you home."

"You better let me out at the bus. You want my parents coming out on the driveway to say hi?"

I was deep in the lying in which I was able to go on. To Tom's friends about Tom. To Tom about Dixon. To Dixon about myself—and the sure-certain collision course he was on at school. Even to the underground where the assumption grew that my taste was for women. This suited me fine: I wore my father's shirts to the parties and taught myself to hold my cigarette like Humphrey Bogart. Lies for everyone. The more I lied the better the picture: my parents saw a wholesome adolescent, a bit bookish, a bit repressed. Not easy about flirting or willing to wear lipstick. Still such a child! But lively. And so well brought up, they imagined the neighbors thinking. Given to bursts of enthusiasm for things the whole community was pleased to brag of: kite flying, for example, folk songs, and, oh yes, French poetry....

RECOGNITION

I was lying on the dry earth in between my tomato plants. Which were just transplanted. A circle of mud around each one. Several drooped over from shock. The plastic baggies I had meant to tie over them lifted and slide further down the row, but the wind was not strong or cold or constant. There was a smell of scorched insulation, a whiff like the scent left when a match goes out. My own smell was acrid, stronger than the dirt. My nose seemed to be pressed against the inside of my right arm. It was preternaturally still: the plastic bags ticked as they settled and I could hear my own breath stirring the small hairs inside my nostrils.

Lightning doesn't strike twice in the same place is a lie, is what I thought. Lightning doesn't strike in the same place twice is a lie.

There was no power to move any part of my body.

—Henry, what are you doing? Why are you standing there? It's going to rain!

Boots creaked on wood.

—Henry! He didn't answer. I knew where he was. He had his outstretched hands on his porch railing, one foot in front of the other like a dimestore sea captain. It was barely forty feet from the back of his porch to my tomato patch.

Is a lie, it continued. Is a lie.

—I'm coming, Henry said. I listened to his heavy feet moving on the porch planks. The screen door squealed and clunked shut. Henry's wife was talking again, but her words were muffled.

Lightning doesn't strike twice in the same place—is a lie.

I was unable to burst into tears, but I felt the terror bursting me. My left side rang like a bell. The sensation went all the way down my left side and into the dirt, I knew that. I knew it was a marvel, and terror hit me again.

And still no rain. The mugginess intensified. Wan sunlight warmed the back of my right leg below my hem. I've never remembered crawling back to the house. I remember being watched by Henry: the sound of his calloused fingers on the porch rail.

—I'm coming, he said.

Don't you see me! You must see me. You know he saw me, or he heard it. It must have thundered as I went down. His feet moved on the wood. I thought about the high white-blue sky, marked with a milky pattern of thunderheads along its western edge.

I dragged my dead left leg up the three steps into the mudroom. The kitchen door was open. I could hear Mother in the bedroom upstairs, and I began to think feverishly how to assuage her anxiety without climbing the impossible stairs.

We drove over to the Boy Scout camp that summer to pick up my brother because my mother saw in the paper that a kid at his camp had been killed by lightning. She was furious: he had been in the tent right next to my brother's, and it hadn't occurred to the camp people to phone the parents or that any of the other kids might need to go home.

Lightning had struck a tent just to the right of the one my brother was in. All six boys were inside when it happened. Maybe the one who was killed had had his hand on the tent pole at the wrong moment. This same dead boy, we were then told, had been struck by lightning on a ball field in his hometown about two weeks before. They'd written him up in the local papers as a miracle.

My brother acted as if the kid's death had nothing to do with him—and why was our mother making such an embarrassing fuss. But she made him come home.

I thought the camp was creepy. The tents were pitched along a rough service road, a long line of pine trees towering behind them, and, in front, a mowed field that ran down about fifty yards to a large pond. Somehow, it didn't make sense. One tent among the thirty, and all those tall trees. Why didn't the lightning go for the tallest tree, or for the pond?

Even though I knew the thought was off, I was thinking of that kid being just a little superior to his tentmates. Mr. Secret. I couldn't help it. I thought of the kid calling the lightning down, down on his indestructible self.

I was almost hit by lightning, and I was inside. There wasn't a storm either. It was just muggy, I mean heavy and impending, like today. I was in my armchair reading—and a ball of fire came through the open window and rolled across the living room floor. I mean it, a great blue fucking ball of fire. I had plenty of time to see it. I think it went rather slowly. And then it just vanished. For a few minutes I didn't believe it had happened, until I noticed the rug. A long black scorch mark ran right down it.

Now that I'm old I know that when I was in kindergarten my perceptions about the children around me, how I could see the reasons why one child was admired by everyone in class while another, seemingly no different, was perceived as simply ordinary—I know now that those perceptions were unusual. I could feel what the other children felt—deep admiration for the leader child, whose very skin radiated the confident rightness of being liked—and also know at the same time, with great sharpness, that this child was at heart selfish and unfeeling, that other less remarkable boys and girls had qualities of tenderness and loyalty she would never possess. But she was blessed. Did it begin with her sureness that our affection was her right? She had our wholehearted approval. We all wished to be like her as well as to be liked by her, even me, with my knowledge of her stingy, stunted core.

I kept very quiet. I tried to make everything work out. I struggled to keep mud from my shoes, disappointment from my parents. My mother, before her widowhood and illness, was a gentle, patient person, who would sing beautifully when she thought she was alone. It was a great pleasure to me (I never told her) to sit on the landing, where our back stairs turned a corner, and listen to her downstairs in the laundry room.

Mother had dreadful emphysema at the end.

It was three hours before I was strong enough to drive the car. I had to leave her alone in the house, with lies and promises. My left side tingled unbearably, and a point just inside my left shoulder, where I'm sure the lightning entered, has remained sensitive ever since. But the doctor on duty in the emergency room told me my story was impossible. There was no sign of a burn anywhere on me.

The next day, there was no evidence in the garden either, not so much as a bit of blackened string.

That was the summer I began spending afternoons in the library. I would look in all the newspapers they had. I often drove across the county to the big library, to look in more, looking for those headlines: *Girl Struck by Lightning at School Picnic, Unhurt* or *Lightning Leaves Man Unharmed.* Then I would write in care of the newspaper in which the story had appeared. I was sure I could find someone like me, but it seems to be something people won't discuss. No one ever wrote me back. My letters were very simple, short, and straightforward.

Mother called, pained and querulous, from upstairs.

—Mildred, where were you so long. I worried.

—Just in the cellar, Mother.

And then:

—Mother, did the thunder worry you?

—I didn't hear any thunder, Daughter. When was that?

But you must. I was only in the garden. There was a bolt from the blue, from the white-blue sky. It hit me.

I don't understand why no one ever wrote me back. I began to think over all my old thoughts. I find I cannot add any new ones, it has been too long. When I wake up, I'm still lying on the dry earth. It never rained, I'm certain of that. Henry never so much as blushed. I thought he would have difficulty looking at me. If I'd died, he and his wife would have waited until the next morning, and even then they wouldn't have gone into my garden. They would have telephoned the sheriff. Oh, long before the next morning, my mother would have panicked and she would have called the sheriff.

Direct lightning strikes to humans usually cause death, and in fact do cause more deaths than any other weather phenomenon. Seventy percent of the deaths are single events and hence receive little publicity. A number of golfers have been killed because their shoes were equipped with metal cleats, making their bodies more effective lightning rods. The telephone is considered by many people to be safe, yet lightning strikes during calls produced telephone casualties of four killed and 36 injured between 1959 and 1965.

We had often exchanged the things neighbors do. News about road repairs, garbage pickups. I lent them a snow shovel once. And when my mother died, Estelle came over with a bowl of macaroni salad. Henry would have waited until Estelle saw me lying there. Then she might have made him go over. But that wouldn't have been until the next morning.

I don't think Henry or Estelle have ever touched my hand. Always a thing, some object, is between us being passed back or forth.

I feel sure I belong to a very small group. If all the survivors in the world were gathered for a photograph, how many do you think we would be? A tennis court full? Surely not a baseball diamond. About a hundred people are killed by lightning every year in America. There's nothing funny about it, yet it often makes people laugh.

I'm not sure any more what I hope will happen should I make an objective or theoretical inquiry on the subject. I don't mention it to anyone anymore otherwise. I understand the connections people make. I know well enough what the young doctor in the emergency room decided about me. I don't understand why I earn such condescension. My mother died almost five years ago. So much that must have happened to me has vanished.

SOME CHINESE PICTURES:
A FAMILY HISTORY

for David Rattray

"I can't remember when I didn't think about my parents' Chinese pictures. They changed positions as our family moved from house to house, but they were always somewhere, and still are.

One of them shows seven horses—a colt, a pregnant mare, a yearling, two lovers, the top stallion, and a very old horse, lying down. The colt and the lovers are occupied with their games, but the others gaze out of the picture, catching your eye in a way that has always made me wonder if I'm supposed to understand something from it. I've seen real horses do this.

In the biggest picture, which now hangs over my parents' fireplace, a great man sits on a porch at a table piled with books. Half of the porch is a geometrical plane of deep space on which stylized chrysanthemums spin. The other half is realistically rendered. The great man is writing, or painting, into the fly leaf of one of the books, surrounded by bending, slope-shouldered women. They cluster at two sides of his table, and stand on the ground in the garden below. Well-educated voices hum, discussing literature, and the unconscious sexual honeybees work the wisteria. The colors are silky greys and beiges, the colors of dry fruit bark, old stone, sand. Tiny bits of delicate embroidery on the admirers' clothing are picked out in pale carnelian and turquoise. These details glow like one open flower on a wet March morning.

In the hallway, by my parents' bathroom, a small figure pours over papers. Perhaps they are maps, perhaps a journal. The man is sitting inside a tiny climbers' way-station but the landscape looks unclimbable. The narrow panel is crowded with grey-brown jags so steep the small trees grow on them sideways, over abysses. This painting is harsh brown and black and grey. There are clumps of spiky texture. And unexpected blanks. If the pines were once dark green, they have been black as long as I can remember. I've seen photographs of mountains in China that look like this, and the first time I did, I was shocked to learn they were real. As a child, I took the image straight, with a child's untroubled acceptance of abstraction.

My sister is uncomfortable with pictures that tell more than one story. That is, the sister I know today. We never spoke about those pictures between ourselves when we were children. She is older. A gap exists between us, but it would take much more than the three years age difference to explain it, if it can be explained at all. Then as now, she readily agrees with our parents in many things, while my objections continue to grow deeper and more irrevocable. Our parents named these pictures, in the original brute sense of nailing down content in order to limit its power. They declared the pictures to be The Literary Tea, The Seven Ages, and Scholar's Rest.

Once, in our grandmother's upstairs hall there was another Chinese picture: two long-necked geese (such soft speckles on their necks) standing in a few clumps of bending yellow grasses. But that one must have been sold by our perfidious cousin when our grandmother's house was dismantled and she was sent to a nursing home. No one in the family has it now.

Long ago, all of these pictures belonged to a professor of Asian Art at Columbia University—they were part of a collection he had spent his life assembling. The professor was a citizen of the world and had been at Columbia for years, but when war was declared in 1917, students rioted against him. Suddenly he was an enemy alien, a Teutonic monster, a Hun. The academic community agreed. He must return to Germany at once. The protests were public. The university complied.

Our grandparents were harshly criticized by their friends for going to the professor's emergency auction. Even attending wasn't patriotic. And they evidently experienced both intense greed and shame, for they bought these pictures and one or two others our uncle now has, for "a fraction of what they were worth," but they left the auction before others which they admired had reached the block, and discussions about these unbought pictures continue, even today, long after my grandparents' deaths. So it must have been our grandparents who created the first strophes of this family legend, but it was embellished and continued by our mother. Aura surrounds these pieces of silk and board.

Another war with Germany was in progress when I first heard this story. I was to take the tale as an important lesson about the dangers of prejudice and mob rule. But we had the pictures. They were works of what mother always called "museum-quality" art that would not have been in our household otherwise. It wasn't hard to see how she really felt: the luck of it!

The pictures have not been well cared for. All need cleaning, rematting, and restoration, especially the large one that hangs, against all good sense, over a frequently used and often very hot fireplace. The pictures will all be left to my sister, it has been decided. She has learned Chinese and become a professor of Asian studies. She has taken her daughter to China twice and is now urging her to consider a university exchange program that will place her in China for a year. I imagine that she too can't remember a time when she didn't think about these pictures.

But I'm not at all sure my sister will take care of them any better than our parents have. To commit actual money to the care they now need would make her very anxious. This goes right to the heart of a family plot about privilege and power and not being harassed; about being taken care of as a metaphor and an actual necessity. Ours is a troubled family. Love of money, never admitted, beats a sullen rhythm in the plots. And yearly, The Literary Tea is ceasing to exist as the chimney heat steadily unlocks the molecules of silk.

In the upper left-hand corner of this picture, vertical rows of characters discuss the concept that style is everything. The manner of the character means as much as its connotative meaning; in fact, contains the meaning. The great man is great, as my sister deciphers the characters, because he is the one who has drawn or painted or written the characters.

Above the scholar's mountain, a thicket of ideograms attests to his desire to know more (to be more aware?) of Buddha and, by implication, to know more about himself and yet dwell on himself less. The space devoted to characters on this panel is so dense and dominant that I've wondered if they are chant, or if they chart an investigation through layer over layer of meaning and identity.

No one, not my sister or any of her professional friends, has ever been able to interpret the few columns of characters beside the horses. My sister suspects that this painting is a forgery, but of course it has now become, in its own right, an antique.

FAMILY PLOTS

...a *vast body of curious beliefs. customs, and story narratives are handed down by tradition from generation to generation, the origin of which is unknown.* *They are not supported or recognized by the prevailing religion, nor by the established law, nor by the recorded history of the several countries. They are essentially the property of the unlearned and least advanced portion of the community.*

It was noted that wherever any body of individuals, entirely ignorant of the results of science and philosophy to which the advanced portion of the community have attained, habitually believe what their ancestors have taught them, and habitually practice the customs which previous generations have practiced, a state of mind exists which is capable of generating fresh beliefs in explanation of newly observed phenomena, and is particularly open to receive fanciful explanations offered by any particular section of the community. Thus, in addition to the traditional belief or custom, there is the acquired belief or custom arising from a mythic interpretation of known historical or natural events.

—The Folk-Lore Society, London, 1908,

the year my mother was two years old. Who is in our family the teller of stories. My father, who dominated all conversation, told neither stories nor jokes, and resisted—cross and irritable, not amused—any attempts of ours or mine to pry out his early childhood memories.

—I fell in a sewer. I think I was seven, he said. —That started my memory.

It's my mother who produced the memory of his rescue from death by diphtheria, when he was, she said, about four. Some sort of horse serum was a last-ditch attempt, and sick as he was, she said, he has never forgotten the entrance of the doctor carrying a hypodermic needle as big as a baseball bat. So we must never think it funny or cowardly that our grown-up father turns white and sweats at the casual suggestion, merest hint, that he might need an injection of some sort. Nor think—for one minute!—that we could use his fear to excuse ourselves from tetanus-typhoid-and-rocky-mountain-spotted-tick fever inoculations, every relentless summer, christ, no matter how it hurt going in, and for days after: a screaming goose egg right over the bone in your own best arm, bad enough to wake you up in the middle of the night if you rolled on it in deep sleep.

Dad's aversion was in a different category.

But—how did she know his story?

If you imagine him grateful for her protection, take care: he is panicked and sere.

She, not he, told us that his grandfather never traveled anywhere without four steamer trucks. Dressing was as mother's milk to him. The flap is echoing still among the women in his family about his starch, his brushes, and all the complex logistics of maintaining his sartorial standards no matter how inconvenient doing so might have been.

But he was a salesman, I learned later, this unknown gent who was the grandfather of my father. Eventually prosperous and promoted to management. Of this there is evidence because the gold pocket-watch my father, unaccountably, gave to my husband, says so: "...your forty-five years of faithful service to the Singer Sewing Machine Company, ultimately and notably as manager of the Richmond South Division...."

Now, do you think a sewing machine drummer on the road on the trains of the post-Civil War South, rode with four personal trucks? How innocent is this story, that it should need to be repeated?

Family. Family. I know this isn't exclusive stuff. In fact, it's a good thing you can't get a word in on this page or I might have to shut up and wait for you to tell your tales. I'd have to wait, quietly—and your stories might be interesting! As it is, though, you can think what you want but as soon as you start reading again—well!

For example: One day, when my husband was a little boy, he opened the door to the bath to discover his father standing up in the bathtub.

—But why don't you sit down in the water? he piped, and his father shouted —Shut, shut, shut up and shut the door! It was his mother who described the brutality of who? a coach? camp director? YMCA instructor? But wait, this boy was in London, in the narrow streets of the East End, in 1908, in a Jewish neighborhood. Forget the YMCA. This is barely   past the time of the Ragged Schools, the same poor, cramped, damp, scramble-on-your-own East End that met young Charlie Chaplin. So where did this scene take place: a swimming lesson in which—one by one—thin boys in baggy cotton trunks are pitched headlong into deep water?

Mark sank to the bottom, eyes open, waiting to be folded into the deep blue apron of his unloving mother. Water swamped his gag reflex; he pissed, faded, and had to be rescued, a model of the failure of the method, a revenge on his tormentor.

Would you be proud of such a moment? Cold in your thin trunks, facing the rotten British Empire?

A singularly listless, gullible, and vindictive man I know has one redeeming feature in my eyes. Typically it isn't actually his. He's the brother of the only student ever to run away from A.S. Neill's famous open school Summerhill— and make it stick. When found and forgiven he refused to return. O Freiheit, in your beauty!

Walking into Mark's living room to fetch my children I heard him at the finale of a story about his great interest in swimming. The narrative featured competitions, medals, honor to the community. —Lost, he said, of the medals, —like everything! to the clamoring of —Grandpa, let us see, please, please, please.

I like the other story better, not because it is more likely to be true, but because it is my husband's story and it is mixed with his electric memory of his father's naked penis, the first adult organ he had ever seen.

—We were the first generation to cast aside these lies about the Jews, my father-in-law said. —Modern! he said.—We broke from the hillbillies with their stultifying superstition. We showed the bigots we meant business.

It was his story. But it is not innocent. I think of a pit or a dike that he patched regularly.

I'm from a place where hillbillies singing in their clapboard church Wednesday evenings made a raw clanging tattoo on my nerves, speaking of the truth of feelings, from which I was forbidden. Their dense clusters of notes, not tidily separated by thirds; their clapping and stomping, their fervor. I was not permitted such excess. We were nice people. My longing included fear. From what dangers was I being shielded?

Only when I was older was I able to suspect the social use of these divisions.

But, once upon a time, dear reader, I was the hero.

These days, I'm told I never tell a story accurately. Family and friends complain. Even so, I've come to bless my traditions: Embellishment. Treachery! The attributes of Saint Scheherazahde. Am I saved yet, sister? Is it morning?

Those Chinese pictures I'm so proud of? I have to confess I described them wrong. I muddled and combined their details, forgetting several of them completely, although I claim to be obsessed with them as the first works of art I ever came to know.

Ours was a modest home, fervently immodest in its presentation of genteel impoverishment as the highest proof of developed intellect and inner values. My life was in danger. We had antiques of various kinds, exceedingly thin silver spoons, battered silver teapots that wanted mending at their spouts, platters, and copper luster pitchers, and a number of Chinese paintings on silk, fine, fine, "museum-quality art" was my mother's favorite descriptive term. These possessions unified all our houses. Houses plural because we moved often. It was serial monogamy, not redundancy.

I'm an inch from telling you about war—World War II, this time—and its dislocations to explain our moves from apartment to apartment and from suburb to suburb. But that's a myth the father-in-me likes to promote. (Oh, how he craves to be linked to the great processes of history.) In fact, my father did badly in the politics of literary publishing in New York City, and he saw conspiracies, Jewish conspiracies, behind his poor grasp of human character and his deep personal fear of money.

These lovely things, the paintings and soup tureens, my mother loved to explain to us, were ours through luck and tragedy. Her stories. Her parents, her family—a not so subtle stab at our dad's ineptitude—her parents amused themselves by collecting copper luster, fine china, good silver—in second-hand stores and estate sales. She presented the graceful story of the Chinese paintings: an awful auction in 1917, when a distinguished professor of Asian Art at Columbia University had been forced to leave the country in the maelstrom of anti-German hysteria that accompanied the entrance of the U.S. into the Great War. Wow, the greedy luck of it!

Last summer, I looked inside a small window-fronted secretary in my mother's bedroom, rummaging while gossiping with her—she was in bed recovering from a bout of fibrillation, lousy valves in her 83-year-old heart—and I found a photograph scotch-taped to an inside wall. She said —Oh Gerhardt. (Did she say Gerhardt?)

It was one of those boyish smooth-skinned Nordic faces that barely merit a razor. Late thirties, perhaps early forties. Blooming round cheeks. Soft hair, thinning on top, brushed back from his brow. Intelligence and ingenuousness in the pale eyes behind his studious metal spectacles.

—Those are his pictures, she said, —the Chinese pictures.

What. Who?

She's adroit, I'll say that, fibrillating heart and all. She changed the subject faster than I could pounce. I meant to go back for the photograph right away, but the next time I looked, it wasn't there. Is my curiosity dangerous? I was relieved to find a fragment of dried scotch tape still inside the secretary. Something to assure me that I wasn't in that old Bull Drummond story about the Paris Exhibition and the hotel room that wasn't. But the story is...a dike? a pit? Is my life saved yet?

When the Yankees took Columbia, South Carolina, who got pregnant?

Who wore the papier-mâché masks of the Cowardly Lion and the Tin Woodsman? The masks are too big for kids. But surely not these grey and angry adults?

Who lost face in a marriage that turned out to have false premises? The patent, it turned out, had never been filed, and the paint turned imperfect and separated.

Who sold off the stocks and who refused to buy a partnership?

The brandy had been removed and dirty kerosene put in its place.

Children, don't mention this in front of Uncle Eliot.

The newspaper morgue, my sister discovered, was not complete.

The only surviving aunt says it's her policy not to discuss the past.

I haven't forgotten the matter of my grandfather's silver spoons. I know there are a lot of grandfathers in this story—mine, theirs, my husband's, my children's. But it's only as complicated as what you're all used to.

Once upon a time my maternal grandfather, the one who collected second-hand treasures, was a young lawyer in New York. He was friendless because his family and university connections were all in the South—in those days thought of contemptuously as remote, dangerously backward, and thankfully defeated—and he was ambitious because his family had been ruined by the Civil War and he was their collective hope of recuperation. For which he had come North, where the money was.

Yankees ran the world then, proud of their sharp business instincts and their stern Round Head ancestors—and still flaunting the burn of a much earlier civil war. Practical to the core, they were willing to use the brains and energy of this Southerner, this outsider, but they were not eager to accept him socially, which might give him access to their marriageable daughters. So the story goes. It was years before an invitation home was forthcoming from any of my future grandfather's employers. Seated at last in a fine family dining room in New York City, and relishing everything the invitation conveyed, he found himself required to eat dessert with his own grandmother's silver spoons.

His story: the family crest was unmistakable. His story: I was raised on the lingering grief of my grandmother and great-aunts over the looting of our family house when the Yankees took Columbia. His story: I now have one up on them, something they will never know. I know them for what they are! Thieves. Arrivistes. Not gentlemen! I can smile and wait my time.

My story: my grandfather suborned and co-opted, dutifully swallowing. (I imagine fruit compote with tapioca.) And suffering the rage of the raped. What a story, I think, magical as a crock of gold, practical as the handle of a spoon engraved with an uprooted oak tree, or a centaur, or unmistakable initials in an 18th century curlicue.

My husband's story: What a piece of smart-lawyer romance. Anything to get a one-up. Stuff of dime novels, honey. You believe it's true? Cavalier horse manure!

It's a Family Matter. The Family Romance. Family Therapy. Family Dynamics. The Family Constellation Theory. It's family skeleton, style, tree, fare, meeting, name, circle. Listen to Scheherazahde. She knows when a story needs another cliff-hanger.

Once upon a time, a boy was told his dead grandfather was an ignorant and spiteful tyrant.

Little pigs wriggled in the straw, their round backs the exact color of fresh pork sausage.

The rug sparkled in the dark bedroom. It was snow, blown in from the cracked window.

Once upon a time, a girl was told that family tragedy was caused because a woman had hysterics about her daughter's pregnancy on the front porch, instead of upstairs, inside.

The denim fly felt thick as cardboard; the fat brass zipper unbearably resistant; her fingers slipping from the metal tab and then—in a blast of salty crotch perfume—his beautiful red dick.

Once upon a time, well inside the Pale, a young woman—barely! she was thirteen—explained to her rabbi that she had been married much too soon. That she could not serve her husband, who was three times her age, because she had fallen in love with another, much younger man, an unworldly student who loved the getting of knowledge and who needed a willing woman to care for him. She was small-boned, fair-haired, and determined to make her story stick. Reason is sweet. Only a rational divorce would absolve this misery—her husband's, her beloved's, and her own. A tiny woman, avid for affection, sexual gratification, and domestic power.

Her story, polished like a silver candlestick, is a family heirloom. So familiar as to invite skepticism. The real candlesticks, beautifully fluted columns set on heavy pedestals, were given away by another mother, deliberately, to spite her son. A tiny great-grandmother sparkling in the night sky.

Once upon a time in the city of Philadelphia, a young woman—barely thirty!—explained to herself that she could not serve her husband, who was more than twice her age, because she had fallen in love with another, younger man, a brilliant worldly aesthete, who needed a woman willing and able to be his intellectual equal. The story follows stern convention; divorce is unesthetic; and at bottom she was at fault, as much for her outspokenness as for her sexual indiscretion. Thus naturally, inevitably, she was found making a fool of herself in the most public way possible. She ordered the carriage to drive up and down the street fronting his house. She would do it all night. She would do it until the horse dropped dead. She would refuse to let the moment pass and accept his message that the love affair was ended. She would twist in her fury like the trapped animals who gnaw away their own legs. And she would poison her children against their father because the life she wanted was beyond her reach. A tiny great-grandmother, avid for scholarship, potency, sexual freedom, and recognition.

◆

Let's begin again. It's yet another evening, and we've finished supper. Let the dishes sit. Reheat the coffee. Remember when. Wonder why. Did you know. How easily we believe. Once upon a time.

Peculiarly open to receive fanciful explanations, a state of mind generating fresh beliefs, entirely ignorant of the results of science and philosophy, not supported or recognized by prevailing or established or recorded: essentially the property of the unlearned, to which the advanced portion of the community have attained, habitually.

A horror of needles.
An obsession with fashion.
A fear of deep water.
An honor to the community.
A love of modern life.
A longing for intensity.
A story to justify love of possessions.
A story that punctures a family myth.
A story to glorify family ambition.
Two stories that consolidate family pride.
A story to explain family collapse.

There is nothing abstract in this language—my octogenarian mother was two years old at the time.

SUBWAY

A woman who is late for an important meeting takes the subway instead of a taxi. She has not ridden a subway in ten years, not since she was a secretary. The subway is smaller than she remembered, and colder. She realizes that the heat is not working in her car; she realizes she has boarded an express and that this train won't stop until it reaches 86th Street. She'll have to take a taxi after all, and go back downtown through all the traffic she thought she was avoiding. Nothing can be done now but wait for the ride to be over.

A man seated next to her is reading from a small notebook. She stares because it is exactly like one she often carries. The crabbed handwriting inside it is very like her own. How has this person come to have her notebook?

He is looking at the same two pages, turning them back and forth. She manages to read by looking down and sideways.

"A social security mom," one line begins. "An American girl who visited China," says the next. He moves his fingers: "I know I'm old. I paid for sex. I get no refund. I have no salt, no soul, no refill."

The man is wearing brown wool pants, a quilted storm coat, a fake-fur cap with ear flaps. He is, perhaps, fifty. He seems ordinary. The contents of the notebook are so odd the woman impulsively takes out an envelope and surreptitiously scribbles down what she has read.

The man, absorbed, turns another page. "God hears me. The death bullets. The fee." The woman is suddenly sure he found this notebook somewhere, that he is reading these pages over and over, trying to figure them out. "Both of us are voyeurs," she scribbles on her envelope. When she looks again, he is on a new page: "More death files, you may keep them, the tainters, the foam."

It occurs to her then that a Robert Louis Stevenson story would begin right here: the story would reveal that her copying has linked her forever in a chain of eavesdroppers, trespassers, and spies, and she wonders why she and her fellow passengers allowed themselves to be drawn in, to pass these sick words on, preserving them. Then she realizes that the chain moves back in time as well as forward—back, it seems to her, to the original writer, who will thus be able to know her.

The man shuts the notebook abruptly and puts it in an inside pocket. It's his own. He has put it in a pocket only an owner would use. And he is aware of her reading and writing. He is perspiring; so is she. His clothing is odd; that is, it was once ordinary, but now it's very dirty. The train slows for the stop at 86th. Predictably, the woman is terrified. To leave is to give him an opportunity to follow. She waits as long as she can before leaving her seat and steps off the train as the doors close. The man is still sitting inside. Back on the street, she hails a cab which delivers her to the building where the meeting has surely begun without her. She tips the driver without looking at him.

LITTLE PHOTOGRAPH

From a distance, a father stands in the sunshine with two little girls. All three are wearing bathing suits, and even in a black & white snapshot, the big meadow and tree-covered hillside beyond are lush with summer green. It is middle-class America. The grass is cut, and all the bare feet rest safely among its blades.

The dad holds his daughters with an open hand pressed flat on each girl's body. I can remember the gorge rising in my throat from that pressure. It did not make me feel protected. Sometimes I couldn't hold in my urgent desire to squirm. If I were without my sister, he would hold me with two hands, pulling my shoulders back to straighten me, his fingers digging into the flesh just below the shoulder knobs.

Years later, at my house in Brooklyn, my father was to grab at our cat to stop her from coming in the house. He grabbed her at the shoulders in almost the same way and she bit him deeply in the soft space between thumb and first finger.

In this photo, my sister clasps her hands affectionately around the hand on her chest. I'm the smaller one, with hands rigid at my sides and my knees locked.

My father, already bald, looks very young. He was twenty-eight when he married my mother. Hannah is about eight in this picture, making him perhaps thirty-seven. My parents' marriage was precipitated by Hannah's conception. Would they have married anyway?

My mother had a leather jewelry case with a false bottom in which she kept a dried rosebud, from her wedding bouquet she told me, and a letter, folded up, which I never read. Years later my sister was shocked that I never had. The letter was from our dad, said Hannah. He wrote how he would have asked her to marry him regardless of the circumstances.

But would she have been willing to marry him?

My father is staring at the camera, which must have been held by his sister, our Aunt Bim. She has placed us well. The sun slants from the left so no one has to squint into the light. We are at Camp Allegheny in West Virginia, where my sister is a camper and Bim an administrator and keeper of the camp store. I'm a visitor, along with our dad. Our brother was born earlier this summer, and he and our mother are in Charlottesville, where she is resting with her mother.

It's wartime—the summer of 1942. People talk a lot about "the war" and live placid lives with summer vacations. My dad and I have come on the train from Lynchburg, where his parents live. It's a two-hour trip and I think we go back late this night. I don't remember staying over. Not until three years later when I'm old enough to go to camp, and Hannah is no longer interested, do I remember the big canvas tents the camp provided, the plank walkways, and the night-long insect noises.

Come in closer on this picture: I look up unwillingly.
My stomach sticks out, stretching my shiny bathing suit, while my sister's stomach is flat. I was already tagged fat or potentially fat by our socially-conscious mother, who lost

her place at the edges of New York society when she married a middle-class intellectual from the South. This loss may not have been fully apparent to her at the time this photograph was taken. During the winters, we lived in New York on the Upper East Side where my sister and I attended a famous progressive private school. But a fiction about our differentness had already been instituted.

My knees are locked and my thigh muscles bulge from the tension. I already need to run away. By the following year, I will have divorced my parents. Beginning in these months, just after my brother's birth, I snapped the bond of belief in their authority. This happened because I permitted myself awareness that the bond was shabby, untrustworthy. This happened because I saw—with knife-sharp clarity—what was missing in their relationship with their new baby, my brother. So often, a betrayal of love is blinding, numbing, but for me it was not. It was a blazing recognition demanding response. The precocious wrench—my divorce—drained more energy from me than I could have imagined at three times the age of five, and has taken me a lifetime to recover from.

Here, in the photograph, I am yet in hand; that is, in a sunny meadow a big hand pushes against my chest. My Aunt Bim is speaking. I hold still. I do not smile.

Porn Theater

i s on the corner I turn between the subway station and my office. Advertises its Triple X fare in pink letters, thirty-five inches high. Last winter's hit was *Eight to Four— For Folks Who Like to Get in Early*.

I altered my office hours, so I could ride when the subway is less crowded.

In the spring, *Wide Spread Scandals* was playing, and now the marquee announces *Wanda Whips Wall Street*.

I hope it plays forever. That whiff of drugs, that tickle of delicious sadism, the implication that the underdog gets control.

I've never seen a good porn movie. Dreary video-tapes of women pretending to masturbate with feather boas. Blurred 16 millimeter fuck films in which one can never lose—I couldn't anyway—the sense of impromptu blankets tacked over windows, of a fan or a heater just out of camera range, working inadequately, of the actors, needing the money, and moved by boredom, dreams of adequacy, or stupidity, or anger.

None of it worthy of Wanda, following how imagination savors all the detail it craves without a reason. Dreaming, say, of a cherrywood table top, polished deep mottled rose, needing no legs at all. No one has to prop the slab of wood on cinder blocks to keep it before my eyes, or help me know that Wanda is forever whipping Wall Street.

And they smile and

tremble, and they weep.

She rends suits, expensive suits, of flannel and tweed, as easily as gauze. Wanda in forever shining tights— above which pulses her pudenda punk-dyed magnetic orange. Wanda with magenta nipples. Wanda glee. Wanda peeing golden nectar on a row of supplicating barons. Obediently their tall cocks bob. Wanda, Wall Street begs for you. Like we always knew they would.

BABS

"**B**abs Nolan," my mother would say in that reminisce tone. "Babs Nolan and I..." And then would come the Stork Club stories, the dancing on the roof of the Biltmore, dating gay men for their good looks and protection, driving hell for leather to skinny-dip in Oyster Bay.

Babs would show up on a visit once in a while—a tired, hoarse little woman, straining to look young. She would park in our living room flirting with my father and leaving cocktail glasses with heavy lipstick marks on windowsills, bookshelves, the bathroom counter. I thought my mother could as well have been a plate of old fish to Babs. Babs would cut her best girlfriend dead to get a smile from a man she met ten minutes ago. I watched her work my father till he looked like a ripe tomato. And my mother didn't do a thing. That's the old, old days isn't it? My mother and her girlfriends were united in their preference for the male and disdain for the female.

But they lied.

If my father wasn't in the house, if no men were visible, Babs and my mother would hunker down in talk so intimate my sister and I would be shooed from the room. Understand, in our home we were permitted—we were expected!—to attend all the performances whether large parties or small, even when the talk was full of dirty jokes, blue language, or the savaging of other people we knew. We were meant to learn to get along in company, to be sociable—and discreet—from the time we were three or four. The talk between Babs and my mother was something else again. Without those visits from Babs, I might have believed that I knew all my mother's secrets.

Babs died of alcoholism in her early fifties. My mother said she was relieved. As Babs became sick and sicker, she was in and out of public hospitals and terrifying government treatment programs. Babs never had any decent insurance or resources and was dependent on whatever was considered the norm for female drunks without any funds. The social connections she had once had were probably gone by the time her grandparents died. The less said about her husbands the better, my mother said.

Whatever Babs lived on wasn't enough to stave off humiliation, my mother made clear, and death is better than humiliation. Did my mother really think that? She hides a lot of old-line Republican righteousness although she thinks of herself as a free spirit. I was a teenager when Babs came visiting and I remember thinking that death before humiliation was the kind of thing used on boys who wanted to escape the draft. Babs was no military hero, and no social protester either. She was just another old blonde with a genteel accent trying to find a man to live on. And death meant dead. I was a teenager and righteousness came naturally to me.

When she heard Babs had died, my mother burst into tears. Then she steeled up and we didn't hear "Babs Nolan and I..." again.

80

Last month, sitting with my mother in the old age home, I learned how the two of them met. I'm used to her stories about the good old days—about parties and pretty cars, wearing dinner dresses, being brought flowers—but this was a different one. It was about her parents not long after the end of World War I, when my mother was twelve and World War I was still called The Great War.

My grandparents planned a family tour of France. April in Paris. Trips to cathedral towns like Chartres. Then all of May they would stay in the countryside. They wouldn't go to a tourist hotel. My grandmother had found an advertisement in an arty magazine for guest accommodations in a chateau.

It won't be an actual castle my mother was told. "These folks have what we'd call a large farm, with tenants, like your Uncle Frank in South Carolina," her father explained. For all he hoped to acquire from European travels, my grandfather was pleased to point out that his family would be considered well-established by anyone they met. Glen Oak with its avenue of live oaks and pastures down to the Peedee River could hold its own with any old chateau.

The plan was for the kind of leisurely visit my Southern grandparents understood. "To get a real sense of France and the French." This plan was also economical, which everyone understood and didn't mention. My grandfather wanted the cachet of a Grand Tour but he was a long way from being able to afford the true grand manner. His brother was struggling to make Glen Oak pay and he was growing a small law firm in New York. It paid to make himself look more prosperous than he was. There was an element of play-acting to this trip.

This is the story my mother told me. It was an amazing performance for her, because her energy is very limited. She's not allowed to drink these days except for a small sherry just before dinner. She was sipping intermittently at a glass of orangeade while she told me this:

"We arrived in the dark. We were two hours late and we'd missed the evening meal. The train from Paris was nasty and everyone was horribly cross. It was cold and drizzling, and the place the driver took us to certainly was no castle. It wasn't even much of a house. It was a kind of farm building, snugged against two large barns, one of which was half burned down. The driveway went right up to the house, without so much as a hedge or a flower bed. It wasn't until we got to the door that we got what the driver was trying to tell: the chateau was uninhabitable. He said, 'Les Boche. Boom.' And he wasn't trying to be funny. Seems the family hadn't lived in it since 1915. The farm was also called Le Chateau. That's where we would stay. At the farm. We could see the chateau building, what was left of it, in the morning if we wished.

"Your grandmother had been certain this rental would be like traveling in Georgia or Louisiana. Back then, a letter of introduction could get a family accommodations with 'nice people' who'd be eager to cover up the financial part of the arrangement by treating you like visiting kin. Well, it didn't take us a minute to realize there'd be no introductions to the local gentry. The owners were nowhere to be seen. The people who met us were a farm couple, doubling as servants, and none too cheerfully. The old man brought us some cold food and just answered in grunts. The old lady poked her head in to look us up and down, and it was clear she thought our late arrival was a kind of character flaw.

"As soon as we were left in the big bedroom upstairs, my parents started to fight. I was in a kind of alcove, just off theirs, with a bed, a window, and a door that hit the bed. There wasn't room enough in it to set down my suitcases, so all our bags had been dumped together in the middle of their room.

"My father was raving. 'Didn't you ask for references!' and my mother was in a state because, of course, she had written.

" 'The Nolan's granddaughter is supposed to be here studying French,' she said. "'The Chester Nolans. A Charlottesville family.'

"They'd been put in the farm couple's own room. When my mother realized that, it was her turn to wail: 'It's their bedroom, James. This is awful. Where do you think they've gone?'

"'My guess is they're sleeping in the barn,' he said. And then he said we just wouldn't stay. Period. 'We'll figure it all out in the morning.' So we sat together on the big creaky bed and they let me have a brandy and water. My mother drank her brandy neat just like daddy. I always liked seeing her do that.

"But sure enough, the Chester Nolan's granddaughter really was there. That was Babs. We met her at breakfast. She'd been stuck there since Christmas and I don't think she'd ever been so happy to see someone else in her life as she was to see the three of us that morning. My parents wondered if she'd been sent there to keep her away from some kind of trouble at home. It would have been unkind to ask for details, I was told. My mother said everyone knew that her parents were unstable. Babs had spent a lot of her life being shipped around from one relative to another. She had been studying French, all right—at the village school. She told me she sat in the back and mostly drew pictures. She'd taken to wearing a big black apron like the other girls. I don't suppose she really had to go, but there was absolutely nothing else to do all day. My parents were sure that her grandparents had no idea what the situation was.

"I went along with her to school that day. We walked about three miles, mostly along a kind of track, I wouldn't call it a road. It ran between farm fields and wood lots. The woods looked really ratty. There were lots of broken trees and we passed signs with black and white stripes and huge red and black letters that said 'Arret!' Babs said they meant unexploded artillery shells. There were crews in the district who were supposed to disarm them, but she'd heard there were so many they didn't know how many years that was likely to take.

"'Once in a while you hear one go off,' she said. 'Doesn't sound a bit like thunder. It's not always one they've set off on purpose, either.' I knew immediately she wasn't kidding. I wouldn't have stepped off that track into the woods for any amount of money.

"The school was just out there, miles from anything. It was a little brick and stucco building that looked like a miniature Victorian factory. There were maybe fifteen children, little five- and six-year-olds mostly—and one large boy with mustache on his upper lip. All in the one room. They sat in double desks. For healthy Americans like us that meant being squeezed in hip to hip, but I was glad to sit next to Babs. The others were sallow looking children with terrible teeth and powerful body odor.

"The teacher kept talking about the front, the front. It took a while before the term sank in. I didn't have very much French. She meant the war. The war was already ancient history to me. At least it had been until I saw those red and black signs on the road. The front, the front, the teacher said. It was ten, it was twelve, it was sixteen kilometers straight up the road, she gestured. My French was getting better by the minute.

"Why didn't my father know how close we were?

"I didn't normally pay much attention to people like schoolteachers. I don't remember her dress or how she wore her hair, but I can still hear her voice. Her harangue was for our benefit, of course. She kept saying how we couldn't possibly know. And tears began running down her cheeks. I wasn't used to adults displaying any emotion stronger than amusement or annoyance. I was violently embarrassed. She stood there with tears pouring down her face and she paid absolutely no attention to them. She kept on talking.

"'Our men. Our young men. You can't possibly understand.' She kept shaking her hands and staring at the two of us. 'They lived in mud. Mud up to their knees, up to their thighs. They were always wet. Years, years. Sixteen. Seventeen. Eighteen. They would march up this road. And the wagons would come back. With the dead. This high! Dead men. You can't possibly understand. They wept. They were so miserable they wept as they marched.'

"There was foam in the corners of her mouth. Some of the younger children were crying too, and the big boy knocked his boots together, clap, clap, clap, under the desk right next to me.

"We took Babs with us and went back to Paris the next day. Daddy got into one of his extravagant moods, and Babs and I went a little mad. We had money to buy leather gloves and handmade handbags. And we went to the horse races, which were wonderful—what a beautiful track. We even hired a car to go way out into the country for a duck dinner—some specialty daddy had heard of. We were the only ones there. We had to wait two hours to eat. They went out back and killed ducks just for us. The dinner was heavenly!

"That's how Babs and I got to be such close friends," she trailed off.

"Funny thing," my mother said suddenly, ending up.

In the silence I could hear the creaking of her plastic seat protector and wondered if she had wet herself. Sometimes I forget how old she is, the bad state of her bladder, her teeth, her heart valves. She looked sad and I kept quiet. I was expecting to hear her nail this box back shut with one of her pet themes, like how much pure luck has to do with one's life because Babs had never found the right man.

"How people carried on in 1940," my mother said after a bit. "France was supposed to be a great country, like Britain or America, and it fell overnight. Almost as fast as Poland. Suddenly there was no one left except Nazis. Paris was gone. We thought it was gone for good, you know. People like your father said it was government corruption. People like my father blamed cowardice and the communists. But I remember thinking about those French soldiers crying on their way to be killed. And those smelly undernourished children. They were the soldiers for the next war.

"I don't know anything military, and the schoolteacher was right, I'll never understand. But I wasn't surprised at the fall. It seemed to me all of them had taken too much already."

CRAFT

When I was ten years old we lived across the road from a young war vet, his wife, and their infant son; they lived in a large stone barn nearly 200 years old, which they were in the process of rebuilding. They called it renovation. Ruth occasionally carried or held things. Arnie did everything else, from the plans he drew and redrew on huge sheets of graph paper to sawing, hauling, nailing, taping, plaster and sanding work. Later, after we moved away, I heard the finished house was an architectural extravaganza, with balconies circling a plant-hung light well, with wide bedrooms upstairs for each of their four children.

When I knew them, no skylights broke the roof. The top reaches of the barn swam with shadowy current bearing construction dust and the twirling blue plumes of Arnie's cigarette smoke. The air never smelled of cooking or house plants but of pine studs and caulking compound. On the ground floor, behind their baby's temporary bedroom, Arnie installed his design studio: a spot-lit drafting table, a padded stool, drawers for finished work, and racks for materials. He had rows on rows of colored pencils in more shades than I had ever imagined were made. They lay in color order—incipient as eggs or embryos. I breathed over them. Respectful. Envious.

Stuart's crib was just around the corner.

While Arnie worked on the building, the space was filled with saw whine, staccato bangs, creaking, plopping. A relentless force seemed to accompany him, as if he worked with invisible companions.

When Arnie worked in his studio, you could hear only the patient squish of Ruth's white shoes she was still wearing from her hospital days. They had met when she was Arnie's nurse.

In the incomplete kitchen, baby bottles aired on small wood pegs. In the noise, the baby slept. In the quiet, a spoon scooped lukewarm Pablum from a thick blue bowl and Stuart made placid baby syllables.

Ruth spoke softly always. She gave me grave instructions in baby handling, let me mix formula, and told me what it felt like to be pregnant. We never mentioned sex or labor. Noise or lack of noise would radiate through exposed studs, where strands of wire and metal cable curled and warm air belched from the raw aluminum ducts.

Arnie was startling in shorts. His thighs looked like winter farmland at 30,000 feet—small square patches of pink, ocher, and tan. He'd been shot down in his bomber, and had fallen in a long parachute-buffered trajectory, burning as he fell. He had fallen into Germany. He told it this way: He was a Jew, falling pell-mell, and the Germans could see him coming like a comet. But instead of finishing him off, they had pumped him as full as he needed from their dwindling stocks of plasma, morphine, and sulfur drugs. His small Star of David remained undisturbed on the thin chain around his neck.

"Y'know, they were losing by then," he told me one day, his eyes hard as a bird's. "I was an American officer—and they were losing." And then, musingly, as he swung his legs out straight for me to see how his scars shone like hard silk, how he was quilted like a lamp shade, "My surgeon was an artist."

What are you supposed to think here, to accompany the images of this tense young man with his unnatural legs and his phlegmatic wife making their life in a looming unhomely space which they—or he?—had elected to transform. Is this a story about craft?

From the same time in my life, as a child not long after the war, I remember someone who had been a fighter pilot in the South Pacific telling my parents how a friend of his had delighted in machine-gunning the frantically scrambling black dots on an open beach below them. The man said his friend had said it was precision work, shooting and maneuvering the plane evenly back and forth until all the dots were stilled. And then, it was an itch, almost a pain, an unbearable need to make the dots stop. The man made an urgent case for it, which I recognized even then. It's always a friend who needs the introduction, the abortion, the drugs.

Martha King's prose/fiction and essays have appeared in *The St. Mark's Poetry Project Newsletter*, *Red Weather*, *House Organ*, *Bomb*, and *First Intensity*, among others. She has published sporadically in the U.S. and European small press, and edited the poetry newsletter *Giants Play Well in the Drizzle* from 1983 to 1993. She is currently director of publications for the National Multiple Sclerosis Society. She was born Martha Winston Davis in Charlottesville, Virginia, briefly attended Black Mountain College in the 1950's, and for the last three decades has lived in Brooklyn with her husband, the painter Basil King.

*For Reviews, Bios
and ordering information
please visit*

SPUYTENDUYVIL **dot** NET

Other books from
Spuyten Duyvil

The Desire Notebooks
John High

Day Book of a Virtual Poet
Robert Creeley

Stubborn Grew
Henry Gould

Mouth of Shadows
Charles Borkhuis

The Long and Short of It
Stephen Ellis

Answerable to None
Edward Foster

Identity
The Poet
Basil King

A Flicker At the Edge of Things
Leonard Schwartz

Cunning
Laura Moriarty

The Runaway Woods
The Open Vault
Stephen Sartarelli

Forthcoming 2001 from
SPUYTEN DUYVIL

Are Not Our Lowing Heifers Sleeker
Than Night-Swollen Mushrooms?
Nada Gordon

The Angelus Bell
Edward Foster

Black Lace
Detective Sentences
Barbara Henning

The New Life
Gary Sullivan

Spin Cycle
Chris Stroffolino

Nine
Theodore Enslin

Watchfulness
Peter O'Leary

06/02/95
Donald Breckinridge

Ted's Favorite Skirt
Reversible Destiny
Lewis Warsh